Along Came a Spider

C.R. GARMEN

ALONG CAME A SPIDER

C.R. GARMEN

Along Came A Spider

Designed by RMGraphX

ISBN 978-1-7337463-3-5

Acknowledgements

Thank you to everyone who has helped me bring this fun tale to life. I would list you all by name, but that would be a book within itself. I'm truly blessed to have such a large and encouraging support system both in person and online. I can't tell you all how much it touches me, and how much I appreciate that push you all give for me to follow my dreams. Without you all, this may never have happened.

Special shout out to my fur and scale babies for being amazing.

Prologue

"Professor! Professor, come quickly! I do believe I have found it!" An English accent with a baritone voice announced with an edge of excitement.

Professor Verne Wilder was leading his group of five researchers through the thick foliage of the Atlantic Rainforest. A drizzle damped their jackets and packs, but the mood was still hopeful as they pressed forward to find a specific flower which bloomed only twice a year. According to the locals they had met a week prior, this flower was one of the most beautiful and precious specimens within their land.

The Professor, a man with greying hair, pushed his thick-rimmed glasses up his nose as he warily waded through winding vines and broken branches lying on the dampened ground. The flower was said to stand two feet high with rainbowed petals and a bell as wide as a man's head. Yet somehow, this massive beauty eluded them for two weeks of their travels deep into the brightly blooming forest.

"Hurry now, I believe our search is over!"

The Professor pushed passed a large bush bursting with fresh and sweet-smelling fruit in tropical orange colors, to a large clearing where the eager and desperate voice awaited his arrival. It was a small hole just inches away from the toe of his boot that made him pause.

The rainforest had a plethora of wondrous plants to study and explore. The ecosystem keeping this vibrant new world alive was something to appreciate and respect, for it housed some terrifying beings which needed to be avoided—poisonous plants and creatures grew within the walls of the forest. Among them were apex predators and mysterious illnesses lurking in the air and water. Already, two former researchers had succumbed to the forests deadly viruses and had to be sent back to the ship for treatment. It would not do to lose any more of their meager party.

Darrell Richmond, a young and sturdy man with a thirst for adventure inherited by his father whose vessel they used to make this long trip, ignored the professor's stop in stride and continued pressing forward.

Verne shook his head but let the group carefully examine their surroundings. The younger ones were much more eager to see the future than they were to live in the present. He would have to remind Darrell about that later when they set up camp for the night.

Careful of the hole and whatever may lie inside, The Professor stepped through the thick branches into a large clearing where his breath was taken away.

Henry Smith, another young and eager student of Verne's, stood a foot away from the most glorious flower he had ever seen. The blush on the petals resembled a sunset starting at the bottom of the bell. The top of the flower bloomed outwards, yawning at the gray sky. It was painted in purple, pink, and orange hues with a thick stock protruding from the ground, and leaves almost as wide as dinner plates.

The Professor beamed brightly, calling back for the rest of the group to join them. "You did, my boy! Well done!"

With a faint blush, Henry straightened his brown jacket and cleared his throat. "We have one minor problem with this discovery, Professor," he stated almost nervously.

Verne cocked his brow as the rest of the team

assembled by his side, oohing and ahhing over the plant before them.

"What is that, my boy?"

Darrell stepped closer to the flower and carefully tipped the edge of a pedal down.

"I do believe it is occupied at the moment."

Indeed, inside the bell of the flower was a mass of thick white-webbing. Verne stepped closer with Doctor Scott, a man nearing thirty with bright blond hair who spoke little but never missed a detail, at his side. The peered closer at the opening of the bell yet could not see a single creature moving or hiding inside of it.

"Are you certain the creature has not moved on?" Doctor Scott asked.

Darrell shrugged with broad shoulders . "I suppose it could have, but this mass is too thick to tell."

Professor Wilder stepped back to allow the others a closer look at the web in question, while he withdrew his journal and a pencil to jot down the findings so far. It was important to remember every detail of this moment for their review later on when they took samples of the plant back to the lab at home. Perhaps they would be lucky enough to harvest some seeds to grow. It would be a long study, but worth it if they could recreate this exact environment and watch the life of the blooming flower from start to finish.

"God damn!"

The professor looked up to see everyone had stepped back with their eyes widened and faces slightly paled.

"I suppose that answers that," Scott drawled as he leaned closer to Darrell who was inspecting his pointer finger.

"What happened?" Verne snapped, making Darrell swallow hard.

"I uh, poked the webbing and a spider lunged out at me. But look, I dare wager he missed me. I do not have any bite marks on my finger," he explained, holding out the finger in question.

Scott took his hand and peered as close as possible to Darrell's tan skin. He turned his wrist this way and that, inspecting the man's hand thoroughly before nodding in agreement.

Verne disregarded them for a moment to look back inside their prize. A jeweled colored arachnid, whose jade body was a wonder that it could have been missed, was already drawing back inside it is home. The size of the spider was a concern but…

"Are you sure you weren't bitten? We have no idea what this creature is. It could be venomous."

Scott released Darrell with a sigh and waved Verne over to take a look at his hand. "I believe it is safe to say the fangs missed his skin. There are no markings on his flesh." He stated.

Verne nodded but was not completely comforted by the knowledge.

"It looks as if we've made two discoveries today," another member of the group piped up.

Verne tucked his journal away, a foreboding feeling still hovering over his mind.

"Yes, well, we best start gathering as much information about these new specimens as soon as possible. And please, all be more careful. The forest hides many secrets, I would rather we did not become one of them."

Chapter One

The edges of winter wore through the massive Muffet estate, turning the lush trees into spiny skeletons with a few dried leaves clinging to the top branches against the bitter winds. The acres surrounding the mansion were hard and browning, almost resembling the high stoned walls wrapped around the property. The gate was rusted over but could still be coaxed to move with the proper incentive.

If not for the fresh carriage tracks rolling up to the barn, the estate would look abandoned. No lights flickered in the grimy windows, and the bug-eaten curtains never seemed to budge from their place.

Eleanor climbed the front steps which had been chipped by past winters and hard rainy seasons, with a tan cloth bag clutched tightly in her hand. The looming front doors no longer bared knockers— those had fallen years ago due to age. Still, it was home and she found the manor enchanting.

As dusk settled over the horizon, she yanked the front doors open and stepped into the cracked and dusty parlor. The house was darker than the greying skies outside, and a chill had overtaken the living space. If they wanted to avoid sleeping in their day clothing, she should start the fireplace within their chambers and the living room now. Yet, logic never prevailed against her excitement.

Today was a special day. Her father, the brilliant Doctor Silas Muffet, had received his newest specimen the evening before and had holed himself away to discover what fascinating qualities this precious creature possessed.

It was said to have travelled far across the ocean from a different continent and was discovered by a team of field researchers. The creature baffled them, so they carefully turned it over to her father's possession. It was on voyage for nearly a month. They expected to perform an autopsy to gather some insight into the discovery. Not ideal, yet still imperative to the job. When their fears were proven wrong, and the creature arrived alive and seemingly in perfect condition, they were both elated.

This new discovery, however, did not stop the chores from being tended to. They needed goods from the town, and it was Eleanor's job to secure them while her father worked in the lab. Now that she had a cloth bag in hand with fruits, bread, and vegetables to feed them for the next few days, she was practically skipping through the manor to place the items away and peek at the new addition to their study.

She lit the oil lamp from the side table by the front door and used it to guide herself through the long halls, webbed throughout the mansion. She could follow the path from memory alone, having travelled it so many times during her life, but Father warned her to always be vigilant within their walls. One never knew what may lurk around the corner, having escaped from the lab.

Her long wool skirts brushed against her ankles, which were encased in tall cream boots that clacked lightly on the wooden floors. Her long blond hair was pinned tightly back in a fashionable chiffon. It was as much for society as it was to aid her in leaning over the jars that would litter the counters of her father's study. It would not do to have something latch onto her hair and hold her hostage. She kept her delicate hands covered with leather gloves, dyed to match the deep maroon of her dress and sensible jacket.

Her father noted many times in her youth that she resembled her mother, who had passed away during childbirth. He said the loss would forever stain his heart, but the blessing he received that day gave him a new spark of life. His little Miss Muffet was as precious to him as his work. She wore that knowledge with glowing pride.

A stop through a servant's door gave her a quicker route into thc large kitchen the estate was blessed with. Inside, dozens of pots, pans, and cooking utensils were hung up and tucked away, clean enough to cast a reflection through them. She placed the loaf of fresh bread inside a wooden bread box, then arranged the fruits in a large handcrafted bowl with flowers etched into the sides. Eleanor darted around the open quarters quickly, humming softly to herself as she placed the last of the produce away. She paused to smooth out her skirts before dashing back out in the hallway.

The door to the laboratory was tucked away in the back of the mansion, made from iron, which was always locked. Only two people had the key to open the opposing door. Her father, and herself. He had given her a copy on her seventh birthday, and she had kept it on her person since that moment on. Even when she slept, it was tucked underneath the pillow she rested her head upon.

She pulled the heavy key from her jacket pocket and slid it into the thick lock. With a twist and a pull, the door creaked open to reveal the long staircase down to the basement, lit up by oil lamps encased in the stone walls. Mindful of her skirts, she closed the door behind herself and made the journey below.

The scent of soil with faint traces of vinegar, alcohol, and formalin tickled her nose. At the bottom steps, a coat hanger stood with aprons, face masks, and thick gloves hung from the stretched-out arms.

The temperature was several degrees warmer than the rest of the house, so Eleanor traded her jacket for an apron and stepped into the low light of the laboratory.

"A proper lady should have no business with spiders."

Eleanor smiled, stepping around a bookcase to face her father. "True, but I have no interest in becoming a proper lady."

Chapter Two

Silas Muffet was a tall and slender man. His dark hair was combed back and greyed at the temples. His eyes gleamed with mischief as he straightened from the metal table that had a small collection of jars on top of its gleaming surface. His face was weathered but warm with a soft smile as he took in the sight of his beloved daughter.

"You should. Society does not care for outcasts, Miss Muffet. To whom would you marry with a fascination in arachnology?"

Eleanor shrugged. "A like-minded individual who does not fear a woman with more to her than sewing and fashion."

Her father chuckled, straightening his cream-colored gloves. "Knowledge came to give birth to fear. Perhaps you would be better suited to a man whose mind is less sharp than your own."

She rolled her eyes and studied a Grammostola Rosea, or the Chilean Rose Tarantula encased in a large glass jar. “Please Father, enough about marriage. I want to know about the new addition to the lab,” she pleaded, turning her jade gaze back into him. It was the only quality they shared, though some would say she also had his nose. What an odd statement. How did you measure a nose to know they were the same?

Her father wore simple black pants with a long-sleeved white shirt he had pushed up to his elbows. His mustache was curled slightly on the side of his lips and neatly trimmed. Again, that mischievous gleam brightened his face as he carefully leaned back on the autopsy table.

The entire room was filled with shelves, bookcases, counters along the far wall, and metal tables puzzled into the free space in the center of the room. Hundreds of jars of spiders, both alive and preserved after life, with labels of their species name and identification numbers took up most of the available surfaces provided. What was not covered with an arachnid had loose leaf paper, leather bound journals, hardcover books, insects to feed their collection with, and quills scattered around with the odd bottle of chemical here and there. Truth be told, it was well organized, just not to the untrained eye. The doctor appeared to be a messy man with instruments for experimentation lying around everywhere, yet everything was in a place it would be kept sterile and most useful to him when the need to use them arose.

Even the spiders themselves had a proper place that kept the most venomous safely contained and quarantined in a carefully constructed room, and which required another key to access. Those currently being studied were typically out by the large oak desk the doctor kept his notes upon. Others under casual observation were placed on deep shelves to ensure the jars did not fall should someone bump into one of the bookcases.

The entirety of the lab was a maze that spanned the mansion basement with tucked away and guarded fireplaces to keep the specimens warm year-round. These fires never went out and were monitored as closely as the spiders were.

While science had not taken a huge interest in arachnology yet, the work performed by the brave souls who entered the field was vital. If they could create an anti-venom to the known venomous spider's plaguing society, it could save countless lives and improve modern living around the world. That was the ultimate goal of the Muffet family.

"Are you sure you wish to hear me lecture about boring spiders all night? Would you not rather practice your needlework in the parlor?" Dr. Silas teased.

Eleanor laughed. "Father, there is nothing boring about your lectures, even if they are not about spiders. You are a brilliant and fascinating man."

Her father winked at her. "Flattery will get you everywhere, my dear. Very well, let me show you our newest guest. Perhaps you can help me name her?"

Her eyes widened. "You mean he is a completely new species? Nobody has come forth with their own brand on the discovery yet?"

"Not yet. We have been given a huge honor here, Eleanor. This will be my greatest reveal yet!"

Eleanor peered on the table behind him, but frowned when she recognized only common hobo spiders laid out. "So, where is she?"

Her father's eye gleamed, as he stepped away from the workstation and headed towards the only other iron door in the room.

"She's locked away with the others. Come, let me introduce to you specimen 9958—a mysterious and deadly inhabitant of the rainforest."

CHAPTER THREE

The key to the venom room hung next to the door on the thick rusted hook. Dr. Silas figured anyone who was foolish enough to break into the room without the proper knowledge of what rested inside got what they deserved when the inhabitants retaliated. The keys were fairly large and slid into two locks. One was a six-foot-long metal bar that barricaded the room, while the other was the lock to the actual doorknob. It took a bit of muscle to slide the bar free, and then more to push the two-inch-thick door open. The weight was to make sure the door closed from the springs by the hinges whether someone pushed it shut or not.

The room was around the size of a servant's bedroom with the shelving units built from stone and seated inside the walls themselves. Only one table was present, which stood across from the entry. It had only a few instruments on it, and some paper to quickly jot down notes as they were discovered; as well as a small tank housing a mouse who was curled up and sleeping in the far corner of the bare enclosure.

Eleanor stepped into the room and glanced around at the tubs and glass jars of spiders on the shelves. Most were hidden in thick webs, under branches and rocks that had been placed in their enclosures, or inside piles of small leaves. A slender, shiny black spider was at the front of her jar, though. The beautiful Latrodectus Mactans whose underside bore a reddish hourglass design.

She had been nicknamed Rose, since her web was discovered in their rose bushes near the property line. That was another very exciting day for the Muffet family and led to a wonderful discussion about how to tell a male black widow from the female.

Silas smiled and walked over the far-right corner of the dimly lit room. Upon the middle shelf sat an unassuming jar with thick cobwebs filling the container. The webbing was so thick it was almost too hard to see the spider hiding in the middle of the mass. 'Specimen 9958- unknown' was stamped on the label at the bottom of the container. The top had tape across the lid to show whether or not the jar was recently tampered with. They adapted the practice in case they came across any spider smart enough, or strong enough, to open the lid itself. Or tell them that someone had found a way into the lab during their travels to lecture at universities across the country. So far neither had happened, but one could never be too careful, as Dr. Silas was fond of saying.

"I will move her to the observation tank. Stay back and remember, your protection is worth more than any grant or study. Push the button if she jumps ," her father ordered. The observation tank was a 30-gallon rectangular glass tank free of substrate or branches the spider may be able to climb. The lid was metal, but Silas' own design with three ways to open the large enclosure. The first was unlocking and lifting the entire lid off, the second and third were smaller doors built into the top of the lid with their own separate locking mechanisms. This allowed them to carefully dump the spider into the tank with a lower risk of the spider jumping onto the floor and having to be gassed. It also made feeding the creature easier so they could observe the hunting habits of the spider in question or catching the spider to place it back in the smaller jars if it was quick and evaded the meshed handling net.

Eleanor grabbed the spider killer from the table. The liquid was held in a round, tinted glass container with a narrow piece of tubing that ran from the silver nozzle to a rubber ball that she held lightly in her hand. As much as they hated killing any arachnids, safety was paramount, and they had no clue what this creature was capable of doing yet. If the theories were correct, then the new specimen could kill them within an hour or two of being bitten. It was not worth the risk without having created a cure yet.

Silas unlatched the small door on top of the tank, then broke the seal on 9958's jar. Quickly but carefully, he flipped the jar over and wedged it inside the lid of the tank. Still, the spider did not fall out onto the glass bottom as Eleanor expected. Instead, it remained safely cocooned inside of its thick webbing. To coax her out, Silas tapped lightly on the bottom of the jar. The sudden disturbance did it and slowly 9958 lowered herself into the observation tank from the thin line of web. When her legs touched the bottom, Silas removed the jar from the lid and shut it quickly.

He stood back with a satisfied nod, placing the jar aside to wave his hand at the glorious creature now fully displayed to them. "Eleanor, meet our newest study, the mysterious yet lovely 9958."

9958 was palm-sized with an emerald green body that measured about almost an inch and a half long with eight long legs that moved gracefully as she examined her new surroundings. When she attempted to scale the front glass, she revealed a dull orange oval pattern with a red dot in the center on her underside.

"What a curious marking," Eleanor mused as she leaned closer to the tank.

"It is indeed. I wonder if that pertains to her gender or is a warning of her venomous state. Perhaps it is even a form of camouflage against the thick, vibrant flowers among the forest floor," her father added as he picked up his notes from the desk. "So far, all we have are theories. Nothing completely concrete."

Eleanor smirked at her father. "Have you gendered it yet? Then why do you keep referring to the creature as a female?"

He chuckled. "Not yet, but I have a good suspicion that it is a woman. I shall apologize to 9958 should I be proven wrong."

His daughter rolled her eyes but turned back the creature in question. "What tests have you ran so far?"

"So far all I've done is attempted to feed it and review what notes the field researchers sent me," Silas admitted. "She rejected a roach but has bitten nearly every insect and small animal I placed in the tank with her—which you can see over on the table. She's highly aggressive but appears to be a picky eater. We will keep her on a mealworm and cricket diet, for now."

"What happened to those she infected?"

"The insects died within the hour after the bite," Silas answered solemnly.

Eleanor raised a brow. "And the mouse? When was it bitten?"

Her father wandered over to the table and peered down at the small creature in question. "Early this afternoon. We have no reaction from him yet, however, his immune system is much stronger than a roach's. We shall keep a close eye on him for the next few days to document the reaction."

"How odd… What did the notes about 9958 say?" Eleanor queried.

"Take a look for yourself, my dear," Silas insisted as he handed her a piece of thick cream paper with three neat creases in it.

Dr. Silas Muffet,

First sightings were made on the North-Eastern end of the Atlantic Rainforest, within the bell of a local flower. The thick case of webbing surrounding this species made it hard to visualize the newly discovered arachnid. Curiously, the second sighting was high within a tree. The spider had spun itself a cocoon-like hide in the bow of a branch. It is theorized that this display of webbing keeps it protected from predators.

The locals have experienced this creature, calling it something that roughly translates to grave maker. From this, we can only gather that it is venomous and has already made many innocents victim to its toxic bite.

Carefully we have extracted the arachnid to study, three days after our discovery of the first specimen, but fear we may not be equipped to handle its venom. During the extraction, Darrell was bitten through the thick leather of his gloves. It was only a short time after that he passed away, sweating profusely with his veins stark against his skin, and screaming deliriously into the sky. While the event is tragic, the family has agreed to allow us to perform an autopsy on his body to discover what may have happened during that horrific time.

It is because of this that we turn over the new specimen to your care.

As always, we will continue to share our findings with you as they come to us.

Take care dear friend,
Professor Verne Wilder
June 27th,1887

"What caused the delirious visions? A fever, perhaps? And he did not elaborate on any more symptoms? That is peculiar. As a fellow researcher, even from a different field, he should understand how essential these details are ." Eleanor clicked as she handed the note back to her father.

Silas hummed in agreement and placed the letter back on his desk. "I've already returned a query about it. Whether he replies with more information is up to him. I would hope he does so, and in a timely matter." Silas paused with a sigh before clapping his hands together. "It matters not, we shall discover all of the secrets this creature holds for ourselves!"

Eleanor nodded in agreement and peered

around the room. “Indeed, Father, we always have.”

Chapter Four

"Good morning, sleepy-head."

The mouse slowly lifted its head to sniff the air as Silas reached in to drop some seeds in a small metal bowl. The creature yawned and uncurled from his position in the far-right corner of the tank. His legs seemed shaky as he warily stepped closer to his breakfast. Silas waited a moment before reaching in and placing down a small drinking bowl with fresh, clean water. The mouse flinched when his hand came back into the enclosure but didn't move from his spot until the tank was empty of other beings again.

One step. Wobble. Another step. Wobble. Another step. The mouse fell on his left side, his chest moving quickly as if the poor thing was hyperventilating.

Silas frowned and knelt down to face the

floor of the tank at eye level. The mouse slowly dragged itself back up and shook its head before starting towards his food and water again. He was struggling but after a few hard minutes, finally made it to his reward. He tucked the seeds away in the pouch in his mouth, then went over to lap at the water.

Once he was hydrated and had his meal stowed away, the mouse turned around and hurried back to his preferred corner to pull out a seed and nibble on the edge of it.

"Fascinating," Silas muttered to himself as he stood back up and left the venomous room. He locked the door before taking long, quick strides over to his main desk. The wooden chair scraped along the floor as he yanked it out to sit in and reached for his notebook to jot down the new discovery.

With that updated, he pulled out the logs that documented the spider's feeding habits while Eleanor prepared their morning tea upstairs. Spiders were incredible creatures who didn't need to eat frequently. Many species of arachnid could go weeks without food and suffer very little from it. However, he was pleased to see that an insect was offered to 9958 every two days.

Unfortunately, the logs didn't tell him if she ate what was offered or not. He assumed she did.

While spiders didn't need a food source often, if the opportunity to dine was presented, they would typically take it without hesitation—with the exception of 9958's disdain of roaches.

The last six days of 9958's travels were a mystery. The logs were updated less and less as the creature exchanged hands from the steam-powered train to individual delivery men until it wasn't updated at all. This was frustrating and almost infuriating as he was sure the importance of updating the book was stressed during its time abroad. Thankfully, again, spiders were hardier than most people gave them credit for. 9958 was fine. For research, it made his job a little more difficult but nothing he couldn't work around and discover for himself.

As he suspected, her diet consisted primarily of crickets and worms during the voyage and train ride. Since she wove webs, he wondered if they should gather some flies for her to try. Perhaps that would imitate her natural eating habits more. Silas wiggled his nose as he leaned over to jot the thought down in his notebook.

The door upstairs opened and closed with the soft clang of metal hitting metal. Eleanor's footsteps echoed in the silence as she carefully descended the stairs. Silas pushed his papers and books aside to give his daughter space as she set down the porcelain serving tray with matching pot, cups, and saucers.

Silas waited patiently as his daughter filled their white cups with red poppies decorating the sides. The set was picked out by his wife before she passed away to use during their celebration of their first daughter. It had become Eleanor's favorite when she grew older and she begged him to not hide the beautiful china away, but to use it often with her mother in mind. He could not say no to her plea. Or any request, really. He spoiled his daughter and was not ashamed of it.

Even through the test of time the design had not faded nor chipped. Eleanor washed the cups with the care one would have in bathing an infant. They were usually stored in a cabinet away from the bustle of the kitchen to protect them from being knocked over and broken by mistake.

When the sugar was added, Silas took his saucer and gave his daughter a grateful smile before blowing on the steam that wafted over the rim of his cup.

"Thank you, my dear." He sighed.

"Of course, Father. What are you reviewing?" she inquired as she attentively sipped her own tea.

"The logs from 9958's shipping. I was hoping it could tell me something useful, but alas, it reveals nothing," he admitted.

She frowned while leaning over his shoulder to gaze down at the notes he had scribbled in his book. “Perhaps it will make sense later when we have done some more of our own studies.”

“Perhaps,” he agreed while placing his cup carefully aside.

“And how is the experiment with the mouse going?”

Silas leaned back in his seat and cracked his neck. “So far the creature has been exhibiting almost drunken-like behavior. It stumbles and falls when walking, and weaves off course slightly when attempting to move beyond the corner nest. That has been all I’ve witnessed so far. I would like to check again before we have lunch for any more symptoms,” he rattled off before taking a sip of tea.

Eleanor nodded in agreement as she collected the tray. “Then I shall be back to remind you of its condition soon. I need to wash some laundry before lunch. After that, I can join you in researching the new specimen.”

“Of course, darling. Do what you must. I shall see you shortly.” Silas watched his daughter leave before turning back to his notes. Admittedly he had little to go on. While he wanted to rush the project, he knew doing so could ultimately ruin any further discoveries and compromise their investigation of 9958. But what a fascinating creature she was! So little was known except she was deadly, and the victims would suffer before succumbing to their ill-fate.

Already he could imagine himself presenting the cure to the board of directors and receiving praise for his hard work. The investors would line up outside of the hall doors, curious about what new information laid inside. His name would be splashed across newspapers once again. Hail the brilliant Doctor Silas Muffet! His genius has cracked another mystery and brought humanity one step closer to safety and security!

Such a sweet dream.

It would not come to fruition with him lazing about.

"Right then, back to work," he stated to himself as he pulled the departure logs closer once more.

Chapter Five

Eleanor shivered as the wind whipped through her thick shawl and rustled the branches of the bare trees behind her. The clouds were quickly turning grey, raising her concern for the horses grazing in the pastures and the laundry she had just hung out to dry. The animals, at least, could run into the safety of their barn. But her father's good shirt would not do well to get soaked again and torn up by the rising wind. She sighed as she plucked the clothes pins off of the line.

She had a feeling she should have simply placed the clothes by the fire. Now she was proven that feeling right. How the weather could change from a bright sunny morning to this dreary and dark afternoon was beyond her. Mother Nature was fickle.

Swiftly, Eleanor dropped the clothes pins into

the basket and started loading the wet garments in carefully. There would be wrinkles in some of the delicates, and she dreaded dealing with that later. She gathered the laundry back into her arms and hurried across the lawn to the manor. The back door lead into a small room right outside the kitchen, where she deposited the load and dashed back out to catch the horses galloping outside.

As thunder cracked and rumbled, most of the beasts turned to seek shelter without her aid. For that she was grateful. The few foals and mares left in the pasture would be easier to round up and herd into safety. Her boots pounded across the grass as she held her skirts high enough not to hinder her steps.

"Come on! Time to go in!" she called out as lightning streaked across the dark sky.

CRACK!

The horses neighed in fear as the gust of wind kicked up and rain sprinkled down around them. Eleanor cursed as she approached the spooked creatures, dropping her skirts to raise her hands to them.

"Whoa, now! Easy! Easy! Come on, go back inside," she coaxed, giving one a gentle nudge towards the barn. Once the first horse of the small herd started, the rest followed. The horses whinnied as they crossed the field and for a brief moment, Eleanor let herself relax and release a sigh of relief.

Another streak of lighting was the only warning she received before the skies truly opened up and released their rage upon the land below. Within a few moments she was soaked, and her boots were sinking into shallow puddles as she ran as quickly as she could to put the horses back in their stables and lock up the barn.

The task took entirely too long, and she was shivering uncontrollably by the time she finally stepped back into the house. Another clash of thunder rattled the windows as she pushed and locked the back door. The fires would need to be stoked and fed so they didn't die too early. But she was tired and cold. If she didn't change and dry off, she would surely catch a cold.

She dragged herself through the hallway and up the main staircase to the living quarters. Her bedroom wasn't far down the way, but it felt as though she had been walking an eternity with heavy laden muscles by the time she pushed open her door.

It was difficult to peel off the layers of her dressing. The boots wanted to cling to her legs like a second skin. Her hair was knotted around the pins holding it in a tight braid against the back of her head. That storm was a nightmare, and not just because it was loud enough to rock the floors of the manor.

Eleanor dried with a towel and brushed out her long hair, deciding to tie it back at the nape of her neck for the rest of the night. She redressed in a warm thick dress with a long brown coat to stave off the cold trying to sink into her skin. Before leaving her chambers, she tossed another log onto the small fireplace at the far end of her room and pushed the log firmly into place at the center of the crackling flame. The rush of heat over her felt heavenly, and for a moment she simply basked in it.

Another crack of thunder and lightning outside brought her out of her fantasy for a warm night in bed and urged her forward to finish the chores. A woman's work was never done. She stopped by her father's room to tend to his fire before making her way back down the stairs. The living room had the large hearth that she would place the laundry out in front of to dry. She coaxed the flames higher, then fetched the basket of clothes and laid them out neatly. Her father's favorite shirt was wrinkled as expected, same with her evening gown.

She sighed in frustration but brushed herself off and turned away from the problem. It could be dealt with later. She made sure the front doors were locked against the wind, then wandered back through the maze of hallways to the door of the laboratory. Most likely her father would be so wrapped up in his own work that he would have missed the sounds of the storm. Still, she needed to check on him and see if there was something she could help with before giving in to the urge to take a nap.

The lamps on the wall flickered as she pulled the metal door open and descended the staircase. The shadows they cast were ominous in the stark silence of the room. Even the faint clashes of thunder could barely be heard through the thick stone walls of the laboratory. Nothing broke the eerie stillness.

"Father?" she called out tentatively as she stepped off the staircase. His desk had been abandoned with the chair shoved carelessly off to the side. Had something happened? She wondered as she walked through the rows of captive arachnids.

"Father?"

She stepped up to the door to the venomous room, noting the key had been moved from its hook. Eleanor frowned as she cautiously pulled open the door. Her father stood bent over the small desk with the mouse's tank resting on top of it. He barely seemed to register her approach; his eyes glued firmly onto whatever it was he was doing.

"Is everything alright?" she asked softly.

Silas continued writing in his notebook as she stepped up to his side. His moment of silence was unnerving and when her eyes settled on the tank with the little mouse inside, she understood why.

The tiny creature was no longer curled in his corner but laying frozen in the middle of the glass case. His long tail had thick veins pressed against the surface of the cooling skin. Even in his face, where the fur was thin, she could vaguely see the outlines of black webbing weaving through his body.

Silas finished his notes before clearing his throat and turning to his daughter.

"You can see what had happened. I was here before his final moments came and I wanted to record as much of the event as I could before I forgot. It was truly chilling, my sweet little Miss Muffet. 9958 is a remarkable, but terrifying creature. Alas, I do not wish to regale anymore until I have had a chance to test the blood of the mouse first. Inside this poor thing are the answers to many of our specimen's secrets. We must act quickly if we wish to see them," he stated.

Eleanor swallowed and nodded. This was the difficult part of being a researcher. Death came along with the job. However, if you were good at your part, that death would not be your own. In the end, as cold and calloused as they may be, it was what a small part of their goal was. To keep living, and with it, bring life to those who may suffer.

If they discovered a cure to 9958, it could change everything.

Chapter Six

"The veins are enlarged, making it hard to get a viable sample from the specimen," Silas muttered as Eleanor placed a microscope on the desk in the main room of the laboratory.

"Do you need a smaller needle?" she asked as she moved a tray of scalpels, tweezers, tongs, and other instruments over to their work station.

"No, I believe I have it now. Do you want to examine the sample first?" he offered as the syringe slowly filled with thick, almost black blood.

"Whatever you wish, Father. I can take the notes and examine the body while you run a test on the smear," she offered.

Silas nodded in satisfaction. "Very well, please be gentle. I do not wish to harm more mice than we need."

“Of course.” She took the dead rodent from his gloved hands and placed in on a metal tray. Silas stepped around her to prepare the blood smear while she gathered his notebook and quill to jot down descriptions of the body’s state.

He was proud of his daughter in moments like these. It wasn’t easy to view a once living creature from afar with unbiased emotions tampering the investigation, but his little Muffet did it as well as he did. She had learned and grown so much. It was hard to believe there was a time when he had to change her bottom and feed her from his spoon.

“The skin lost its elasticity to show signs of dehydration,” Eleanor stated softly as he adjusted the microscope.

Silas paused. “I saw the mouse drink heartily this morning. That should not be possible.”

“I am sure the blood test can tell us for certain, but there are several signs that back up my claims present already. No signs of water or wetness around the nose or eyes. I can do a urine test as well, but you said that he was acting drunkenly this morning. Perhaps that was a sign of confusion from the illness,” she mused.

Silas placed the slide under the scope with a soft hum and adjusted the lens again.

“You may be right, my dear. Go ahead and start the autopsy while I run these samples through.

Unless, of course, you would rather I do it?"

"I can start it right now," Eleanor reassured him with the soft clang of metal tapping against metal.

The cells came into focus, a mix of purple and red like circular shapes. The red cells had a deep red outer ring with a lighter almost white middle, while the purple ones were deep in color throughout the entire cell. The red ones dominated the field of vision, with only two white—purple looking from the dye—in the cluster. This wasn't necessarily concerning for the first look, as most healthy individuals had three to maybe four white cells in each field of vision on average.

Silas leaned back to mark the findings on a piece of paper before adjusting the scope to look at another field. The silence was comforting as they worked, with only a soft clang of metal or scratching of quill on paper interrupting the otherwise quiet room.

Three white blood cells. Silas moved the lens again and counted. Four. Then two, again.

He paused with a frown, seeing only two white cells in two different fields was odd. He replaced the slide with a new one and peered down at the sample.

Four.

There wasn't a consistency to the low white

cell count. That would definitely be interesting to test again and review with a new source.

"Definite signs of dehydration, Father," Eleanor stated softly, following the sounds of paper rustling. "And signs of a heart attack. I fear that could explain the cause of death rather than succumbing to the venom."

Silas frowned. "But what caused the heart attack?"

"It's hard to say. Rodents are susceptible to these problems as well as a long list of heart-related diseases." Eleanor worried her bottom lip as she looked back over her notes. Honestly, she did not have a lot of new information presented. Just theories that could be debunked as part of the mouse's genetic heritage.

"True enough, then I believe we should finish this up and move on to the next phase. Getting a sample of the venom to look at directly and introducing it to a stronger specimen. Perhaps the horses will develop antibodies naturally with a small amount of venom given to their systems the same as they have with our other specimens. With that, we can begin creating the cure while continuing to study 9958's workings," Silas mused while rubbing the back of his neck.

Eleanor nodded, placing her instruments aside and wiping her gloved hands off on a spare piece of cloth.

"I agree. I can prepare a light dinner for us to review these findings if you would like to finish up here?" She offered.

He sent his daughter a bright smile. "Absolutely. Thank you, Eleanor. I do not know what I would do without you."

"It's my pleasure, Father."

Chapter Seven

A few weeks later their theory of antibodies was proving successful. In small quantities, the horses were creating a natural resistance to the venom that flowed through their veins. However, they still experienced lower amounts of pain and distress that was prevalent in the mouse who had been bitten head on. This could not do. A cure may be tampered with if the human's, or animal's body was focused on elevating the delirious state it found itself in and creating a new stress to the already hyper-extended mind.

Stress did not aid in healing. It complicated an already complicated process. The symptoms needed to be addressed before or with the cure as its own separate issue to give the victim the best chance at survival.

Due to this discovery, Silas was working

diligently in the lab on a substance that would alleviate pain and the muscle cramping that could cause heart failure as it, unfortunately, did with their test on a healthy and sturdy pig.

Eleanor held the first attempt at combining these medications together in her hands as she approached the stables. She had faith in her father's work but understood cures were only found through trial and error. Her job now was to watch test subjects number one through three to see if this medication worked, and monitor the growth of antibodies being produced for the anti-venom itself.

Despite how small this job seemed, it was imperative to the project. Her hands shook with growing excitement for the possibility this discovery could have for humanity. This serum could have other applications outside of an attack by specimen 9958 if it worked.

The majority of the horses in the stables were undisturbed by her appearance. The ones in stalls marked with numbers 1-3 on the doors with thick black ink appeared more anxious, not that she could blame them. The barn held 13 horses in total, two of which were younger and still housed with their mothers in the widest stalls at the back of the building. The smell was not pleasant, but the floors were kept as clean as possible. Mucking the stalls was another task she was hesitant to jump straight into and wished often they would hire a helping hand to tend to the beasts.

Science was not for the faint of heart or easily bothered. It required a vast amount of hard, manual labor. Though her father tended to do most of those chores himself, lest he was buried in a new project.

Doors one, two, and three were near the front doors with thick padded locks to prevent the animals from accidentally escaping when spooked. She drew out the proper dosage from the small vial of medicine before unlocking the first door and stepping in with the horse. The creature whined and trotted in place with a huff. His large eyes twitched as she carefully moved around him to his flank while whispering soothing comforts and stroking his fur. His head turned to watch her as he stomped his front hoof again in protest.

"I know, sweets, but this should help. Be good, now, and you'll receive a nice treat when we are done," Eleanor promised as she inserted the needle into his hide and pushed down the plunger. The horse neighed but remained still as commanded until she was finished, then stepped aside from her in what little room was left in the stall.

She smiled at him and left, pulling a carrot out of her apron's pocket to toss inside before locking the door.

"Good job, you did very good with that," she cooed.

The second horse went just as well, but the third behaved too erratically for her to dare try giving the serum. His hooves shot out and pierced the air with a loud cry of warning when she stepped up to his gate. His head shook back and forth as he landed with a thundering clomp on the ground again. His nostrils flared with a grumble and snort.

Eleanor worried her bottom lip as she slowly backed away from him. Was it too late to administer the medication? Was something going wrong with their experiment?

She shook her head and decided to note the changes in behavior, but not fret unless it was repeated again in the future. This could merely be a bad day for the poor thing. One thing was certain, a blood sample would need to be procured soon to tell for sure what was happening in stall number 3.

The horse neighed again, lashing out with his hind legs at the back of his stall.

But that sample would be gathered another day. For now, she would let them all be and return to the manor. Yes, she thought as the creature eyed her like a delicious snack. Heading back inside sounded like a marvelous idea.

CHAPTER EIGHT

Silas was working late into the night, refining his medication to combat the symptoms of 9958's venom. After Eleanor gave him an update on how the horses were doing, only number 3 missing his dose of serum, he felt encouraged to double down on his research for the cure.

The antibodies were growing wonderfully. The horses were truly remarkable with a strong immune system that could help them bring an end to the terrors reigning over the locals of the Atlantic Rainforest. However, the formula was quite difficult to narrow down. His theories did not match one another on paper. He could not begin to take those equations and experiment with them until something finally gave and lined up correctly.

But what was wrong? Silas groaned as he

tossed his notebook back onto the desk and ran a hand through his hair. The math had to be wrong somewhere.

Giving up for the night on the conundrum that eluded him, Silas tidied up his research notes and closed his ink pot. He stood up and turned to the stairs when his eyes wandered back over to the venomous room. He had spent a lot of the past two weeks slipping in and out of that door to check on 9958's state and run experiments that have helped lead to the breakthrough in medicine to combat the symptoms his new addition inflicted.

Perhaps drawing out one more vial of venom before retiring for the night would not go amiss. Surely it would make tomorrow's studies quicker to have the task already completed. Since he had to go into town, the time he had to study would be cut short anyway.

Silas strode towards the thick door and pulled the large rusted key from its hook. The locks clicked free, and he stepped inside the dimly lit space. The few specimens they had were quiet and unmoving, presumably content with their feedings earlier. Still, he could feel each of their eyes trained on his form as he crossed the room to 9958's shelf.

It was unnerving.

With a steady hand, Silas removed the jar

from the shelf and broke the paper seal on top. He carefully placed the jar inside of the observation tank before uncapping the enclosure to release the spider inside. At first, 9958 remained immobile and hidden with her thick webs. Being as gentle as he could, Silas gave the jar an encouraging tap on the bottom of the tank. The shadow inside moved an inch. Another tap and the beautiful beast emerged from the jar with her front legs held up high.

"I'm sorry, my dear, but I am afraid that I need your assistance again." Silas chuckled as he withdrew his hand. The spider spun in a slow circle to face him.

Making sure that his thick gloves were secured on his hands, Silas grabbed a small mason jar with a piece of rubber stretched across the top of it and lowered it cautiously into the tank. Before the jar touched the bottom, 9958 lunged at his wrist. Her legs latched onto the leather material protecting his body as she bared her fangs. Silas jerked back, knocking 9958 off of his hand abruptly as he dropped the jar and pulled his hand back as quickly as his heart pounded in his chest.

9958 seemed unaffected by the fall, raising her front legs again as she kept the doctor within her limited sights. Could she even see him? It should be impossible, yet as he held his hand close to his chest, he swore that 9958 was watching him as intently as he watched her.

Their vision was poor. His mind must be playing tricks on him from the lack of proper sleep.

Shaking slightly, Silas pulled his gloves off and tossed them on the small table in the room to examine his hands. The flesh was unmarred by her attempted bite, but it was too close to his liking.

Next time she may not miss.

Silas took a moment to regain his composure before grabbing his gloves and sliding them back on. He snagged 9958's jar and a pair of tongs. This time his hands wouldn't be anywhere near her until she was contained again. The venom sample could wait until another day.

Using the tongs to gently tap the back of 9958's back legs, he managed to coax her back into her jar and tipped the container up to keep her inside. His heart began to race again as he pulled the jar out of the tank and rapidly replaced the lid on. He tightened it as much as he could muster then added a fresh seal around the lid. The shadow of 9958 sat within the center of her webbing, seemingly tranquil as he placed her back up on the shelf for the night.

Silas stared at her a moment longer, wondering what it was she saw through the safety of her cocoon. One jade leg broke through the white strands and tapped the front of the glass.

You.

Silas laughed nervously to himself as he pulled off his gloves.

"That's quite enough for one night. Time for bed," he stated, tossing the fabric back on the desk as he turned to leave. As the door to the venomous room closed and locked once more, those pair of gloves sat lifelessly on the desk top in the shifting light of the torches.

With two tiny holes punctured in the surface.

Chapter Nine

The soft golden rays of the early morning sun filtered through the gap of the thick green curtains in Eleanor's bed chambers. The warmth from the previous night's fire had died long ago, and though the light tried to rouse her from her slumber, she was quite reluctant to leave the pile of quilts upon her bed. Her eyes fluttered open with a heatless glare at the towering arched windows along her wall. It was not the morning's fault she was tired from staying awake so late, nor was its autumns fault for the present chill in the house. Again.

She sighed heavily and wiggled her toes. It was her duty to start the fires of the morning and provide breakfast for her father. He was a very busy man, after all. He shouldn't be bothered with such menial tasks. Still, it was excruciating to take that first step out of bed. Her socked feet touched the icy wooden floors and immediately she regretted waking so early. The quicker she worked, the sooner it would be warm. So, despite her internal groaning, she dressed in a woolen green gown and slipped on her brown boots and set off to light the fireplaces in the main room and dining room.

Once the wood was crackling with little flames that licked across the dried bark, she moved into the kitchen that housed a pile of dishes in the sink from the night before. Chores often went amiss in the Muffet household, but they weren't slobbish. While she may forget to dust or allow the laundry to pile in a basket, they kept the place tidy enough for rodents and pests to stay at bay. Except for the friendly spider or two, they were always welcomed with open arms.

The options for breakfast were still plentiful, and the ideas tickled at her mind until finally she settled on some oatmeal with sliced apples and raisins. It was one of their favorite autumn morning meals—a tradition started by her mother long ago to welcome colder seasons. As an added benefit, it required very little effort and freed up more of the day to pick up where she had slacked before. Or to put everything off just one more night to go back into the lab with her father.

The latter was far more appealing.

As Eleanor finished setting their places at the large dining table with an orange runner that had seen better days, Silas came blowing into the room with a grand smile on his face. He was dressed in black pants with a dark blue shirt tucked in, and a dashing vest with his pocket watch tucked neatly in the breast pocket. His mustache was combed with a soft curl at the ends, and his hair had been tamed back from his eyes. He adjusted his sleeves, checking that the cufflinks were fastened correctly before eyeing the spread his daughter laid out.

"Thank you, Eleanor, your cooking is divine. But I must hurry, I am meeting with Mr. Meyers in town to discuss the new grant for our studies."

She nodded and waited until he was seated before taking her own. The bowls still steamed with the carefully diced apples laid on top of the thick, creamy oatmeal. Cinnamon and butter filled the air as they grabbed their spoons and took delicate bites.

Eleanor waited until she finished the first hot, delicious bite to ask, "do you think it may be rejected?"

Her father shook his head as he swallowed. "Of course not. I have a notion the board will find this case as intellectually enriching as we do. It is all about the paperwork, really, and Mr. Meyers has been gracious enough to lend me a hand in completing it."

A tiny movement caught their eye. At the far end of the table a small spec, barely bigger than a fingernail, scurried across the table top. Silas grinned. "Parasteatoda tepidariorum, a good omen. By the end of the day, we will have our grant and can update the lab!"

Eleanor giggled as she watched the tiny common house spider disappear over the edge of the table. "Then I will begin cleaning to make way for the new equipment," she offered, finishing her bowl of oatmeal.

Her father's eyes gleamed with pride as he stood up and straightened his vest. "That's my girl, I will be back this evening." He rounded the table to place a quick kiss on top of her head. "Make sure to keep everything locked up. We will celebrate as soon as I return."

Eleanor escorted him to the front door where he donned his woolen coat and top hat. With another chaste kiss to her forehead, he stepped out into the cool morning and left. With a forlorn sigh, she pushed herself away from the front door and set about her tasks.

Since the manor belonged to the two of them for years, most of the guest rooms remained locked and abandoned to age. The linens had been removed and the furniture was covered with thick tarps, but it was pointless to keep them free from dust or dirt. They rarely had any visitors who stayed more than a few hours.

The main hall and parlor needed to be swept. Same with the dining room, the kitchen needed to be cleaned up, and the staircase to their private chambers cleared of mud from their boots. Eleanor did not mind doing the cleaning for their home, but the list continued to grow in her mind as she gathered the broom from the closet, and that ever-growing list was becoming daunting. Her father was very lenient on the household duties. It was because of that she would grimace but give the main areas a good shine.

First, she needed to go out into the barn and check on the horses. Donning a coat to combat the chilly wind blowing outside, Eleanor gripped the knob of the back door and tugged it open. The wind blew around her in welcome to the looming winter on the horizon. It would be very soon now.

The trek to the barn left her fingers bright red and shoulders shivering. The temperature was almost too harsh to let the creatures out for a morning run. She made a mental note to pull down their blankets and shake them out before the end of the week. The horses would need it while the snow covered the earth.

The creatures inside were quiet and content,

except for one who neighed and lashed out against the walls of his stall. Number three was still acting erratic and it made her heart drop. He had yet to receive the medicine, which seemed to have worked on the others if their calm demeanor was any indication. Though their eyes did roam constantly around the room as if unsettled by what lurked in the bouncing shadows cast on the walls.

Perhaps it could do with a fine tweaking then.

Unfortunately, with number three thrashing about, she did not dare risk her limbs to inject the horse with the current serum. They would have to continue waiting and watching what developed as time went on. It would be nice if she could catch him when he had tired himself out. Then she would be able to sneak in and alleviate his suffering, if only by a small measure.

"Would anyone care for some breakfast?" she asked aloud as she grabbed a bale of hay from the back. It was heavy to lug around, but the horses appreciated her efforts with neighs of joy.

She smiled up at each long face. "That's what I thought. Time to eat!"

Chapter Ten

Eleanor stared out the front window, worrying her bottom lip. The sky was dimming as the sun set on the far horizon and her father still had not returned from his trip. The nearest town was only a few hours journey by horse. Then the paperwork should have taken up the afternoon. He was set to return by dinner, or the beginning of sunset at the latest. What held him back? Did something go awry with the business meeting? Did something happen to him?

The last thought sent shivers down her spine. She could not imagine a future without her father in it. If someone had assaulted him or if he suddenly became ill… She would not think of it. Negative thoughts allowed negative events to occur.

Perhaps he stopped at the local tavern with

Mr. Meyers before departing. That would make him late to return home.

Harmless.

Not much of a distraction.

Surely, he would come galloping through the iron gates at any moment…

One minute ticked by. Two minutes turned into ten. Eleanor started pacing the freshly scrubbed floors while fussing with her skirts absently. Perhaps he drank too heavily and was forced to spend the night in town? Plausible, her father was not much of a drinker. That would mean she had nothing to be concerned about till the next afternoon. Still, the theory did not sooth her frayed nerves. If only they could instantly communicate with one another. That would be much more convenient than wondering about the main halls of the manor in a tizzy.

And the spiders…

Her eyes slid down the only hallway that led to the lab. Had they been fed? Each one was on a strict feeding schedule that must be maintained no matter what. What about their newest addition? They had not been able to coax it into eating the last night. Did her father successfully feed it this morning? Would the poor thing starve from her naive neglect? She wished he had left a note in case of a longer absence.

Certainly, it could not hurt to check the lab, right? Maybe there was a note in case of an emergency left behind on the study desk. Even if there was not, there was no harm on peeking in on the specimens and making sure they were all doing well.

Before consciously realizing it, Eleanor was halfway down the hall with her right hand palming the thick key from within the pockets of her skirt. She approached the door and hesitated for a moment, then slid the key into the lock and pushed the heavy door open. The silence was eerie as she carefully made her way down the wooden steps into the laboratory. Everything looked untouched as she switched her jacket for an apron and readjusted her leather gloves.

The tarantulas were on the schedule to be fed today but it was hard to tell whether or not it had been done. The long, metal tongs used to drop the insects into the specimen's jars were washed and hanging up on a small hook by the mealworm boxes. None of the spiders had any body parts or carcasses lying in their containers, but that was not necessarily unusual for feeding day, either. Typically, the insect was devoured in a few minutes after being introduced to its predator. Why did not they have a written record to note each day the spiders were fed and by whom? One would think that would be a must for a team of arachnologists.

Eleanor heaved a sigh as she continued to inspect each shelf, and every jar within the laboratory until she stood in front of the quarantined room; home to the most dangerous and toxic spiders they had found thus far. Her eyes drifted over to the heavy skeleton key as she nibbled on her bottom lip.

Just one quick little peek. For the spider's sake, of course.

Her pulse quickened as she unlocked the door and pushed it open with a grunt. The room was dimly lit. Two of the four lanterns had run out of oil during the day. Thank goodness she came inside or else the room would be pitch black when her father came back. That would not do. And while she was refilling the lamp she may as well check on 9958 to see if she was adapting to the new enclosure well.

Eleanor carefully extracted 9958's jar from its shelf and brought it over to the flickering light. She squinted as she attempted to peer through the cloud of webbing taking up the entire space of the glass container but could not see the jeweled spider no matter how hard she tried. With a frown, she gently turned the jar in her hands before realizing the seal over the lid was broken. Her father had not forgotten to replace it in his haste, had he? They made sure to follow all of the proper protocol the night before, but the proof of neglect was in front of her eyes.

Fear tickled her stomach, had the creature escaped? Her hands shook slightly as she settled one palm over the lid. It felt secure, but that did not mean the spider was still inside. She licked her lips, debating on what to do. Replace the jar and pretend she never saw its condition until her father returned, or open it and see if 9958 was still inside?

If she had escaped, Eleanor was in grave danger and would not know it. If she was simply camouflaged in the web, Eleanor would be in danger by opening the lid. Her options weren't promising, but did not risk come with the profession? If she truly wanted to follow in her father's footsteps, she would need to find her bravery and do what was needed for the field.

She swallowed hard and untwisted the cap. With a deep breath, she pulled it away and peered inside the webbing. Again, she saw nothing but a mass of white. Lid glued firmly in her hand she dared to poke the top of the spider's nest. Nothing. Now Eleanor was growing irritated and afraid. Was the spider merely sleeping? Hiding? Playing with her? Did it roam the halls of the manor unchecked?

Her pointer finger reached in the mouth of the jar again when she caught a flash of green and quickly pulled back. The spider sprung suddenly from the middle of the nest with its pincers opened wide. She half screamed as she slammed the lid back on the jar and twisted it with shaking hands. She could not muster the care to worry over whether or not one of its legs got caught when she recapped the container, nor whether the darn thing's face was alright when she all but smashed the door shut on it.

She did, however, take care when placing it back on the shelf before rushing back over to the light. Her left hand tingled, and as she examined her pointer finger, she discovered two tiny punctures in the leather. As if mini, hot needles had met the material. Her heartbeat was thundering in her ears as she slowly pulled the glove off and looked at her skin.

Venomous. Deadly. No cure. Her mind whirled with terror, almost unable to focus on her own unblemished flesh.

Eleanor froze, blinked, then looked again closer to the light. No matter which way she turned her finger, the skin was the same. Pale and unmarred.

Relief rushed over her as if carried by the tides, knocking her legs out from beneath her.

The creature only snagged the leather, not her skin. She was safe and sent a silent thank you to the Gods above for the miraculous miss.

Eleanor took another moment to gather her wits before dragging herself back up and fetching a new label from the drawer of her father's desk. Quickly she replaced the old seal on the jar—which was free from dangling appendages—and left the lab. She would wait for her father to get home before venturing down again.

Chapter Eleven

Silas cracked the reigns as he guided the horse down the dirt road, holding himself up from the unforgiving saddle as they rode faster down the hill nearly half a mile from the estate. His heart was pounding, and adrenaline poured through his veins. He trusted his daughter and knew, logically, that she would be fine without him at her side for a night. Still, the need to get home was pounding on him so heavily that when the wind ripped his hat from his head, he simply ignored it and pressed on.

"Faster, Marshall, faster!" He cracked the reigns again and the horse cried out as it pushed itself as hard as it could.

He should have left sooner, but Mr. Meyers had a new scientist from another country over and wanted them to meet. The group of them spent hours discussing the schooling they had received and how much more they had learned from being out in the field. And about how science was growing and improving every day. Soon, they imagined, the world would represent a utopia that did not resemble the planet they currently inhabited. The cures they could discover, the help they would invent to make life easier to live! It was inspiring to be surrounded with like-minded visionaries who believed an arbitrary box did not exist but only served to limit them so they could be governed by a greedy horde until they passed.

During the conversation Mr. Meyers had brought out a bottle of his well-aged wine and poured a generous round for them all to drink. This was his second mistake, as after the second glass he began to feel ill, yet, not wanting to be a burden on his gracious host he finished the third that had been offered. Next thing he knew, it had grown dark outside and he was tearing down the cobblestone front path to the stables where his steed awaited.

Now, he was racing to get to her and apologize for the oversight. She would forgive him, he knew, but it was time to go back and right the mistake he carelessly made.

Silas cracked the reigns one more time, "faster!"

***

His boots pounded the cobblestone leading up to the front doors, where he pushed them open with nearly enough force to have them bounce off of the walls. Perhaps his urgency was a bit much. What was he worried about? The muffled sounds of bowls clunking around echoed through the manor as he gazed around at the polished floors, and swept steps to the second floor. The house was in fine condition and his darling Miss Muffet was either just finishing her lunch, or almost done preparing it.

He smiled with pride as he removed his riding jacket and closed the front door. He exchanged his boots for more sensible shoes and then set off to the dining room. Eleanor was eating a bowl of something at the far end of the table. In one hand was her spoon, and the other held a book. He chuckled softly, that was his daughter. Her thirst for knowledge knew no bounds.

"What is on the agenda today, Little Miss Muffet?" He asked, taking a seat across from her. She startled, placing the book down before blinking up at him and offering a dazzling smile.

"I was doing some light reading with my snack. How was your trip?"

Silas steepled his fingers and leaned on the table, his lips pulling down into a slight frown. "I am sorry, Eleanor. I allowed myself to become distracted and missed my chance to ride home with the evening light. I left as soon as I could, but still it must have filled you with such distraught. I did not mean for you to suffer with that. It was selfish and—"

Eleanor reached over to touch his hands, stopping his ramblings with a patient smile. "It is quite alright, Father. I can manage a single day alone. Now, please tell me, does that mean everything went well?"

He took her hand into his own and nodded. "You are much too kind. And yes, it went very well! Mr. Meyer's is excited to follow our progress as we learn about 9958 and present the findings to the board. With luck, we can give a cure to the venom this little creature contains to the tribes within the rainforest. It'll be one less thing they need to worry about for their children."

Her smile transformed into a glowing replica of her mother's. It was as beautiful and blinding as the sun. "That is excellent!" She gasped.

Silas released her hands and settled back in his chair. "Now that business is out of the way, what was for dinner?"

A deep blush swept over her cheeks. "Forgive me, Father, but I did not know when to expect you, so I only made a bowl of curds and whey for myself."

He chuckled and waved his hand to dismiss her worry. "I shall take an apple to my chambers. I am afraid travelling has me feeling a little under the weather. Could you wake me in the morning when you arise? I want to get back to our studies as soon as possible."

"Of course."

"Thank you." Silas stood up and turned for the door of the kitchen. He walked the short distance to the doorway before pausing and looking back at his daughter who had picked her spoon and book back up. He smiled and started to turn away again when something caught his eye. A bright green spider was slowly lowering itself from the ceiling above her, with an orange circle on its underside that had an emerald dot in the center of it.

His heart sped up as he reached out and screamed in warning, "Eleanor, move!"

She looked up at him as 9958 landed on her shoulder and… She screamed in pain. The world around him went black. He failed her. His daughter was going to die. *How did this happen?*

Chapter Twelve

Eleanor waited at her father's bedside with a damp, cool cloth in her hands. She pressed it to his forehead again, hoping the fever would break soon. He was sweating profusely, soaking the sheet she draped over his body after she managed to pull him up into his bedchambers. It had been a struggle. He was twice her size and weighed more than she could lift. She grimaced to remember how many times she nearly dropped him when he suddenly writhed in her arms, or how many times she accidentally knocked his feet on the corners of the walls and doorways.

He was looking better, though. His lips were a pale pink instead of the ghostly white they had been when he initially passed out. What still concerned her was what caused him to collapse. It seemed he had been trying to warn her of something, but she never found the threat he believed existed. Perhaps it was part of the fever? Had he caught a cold during his trip into town? Did she need to send for a doctor yet?

He had been sleeping for almost two hours. Eleanor worried her bottom lip as she dipped the rag back into a small bowl of water and rang it out. Just a little longer. If he was not showing signs of improvement by the morning, she would send for help.

Some soup would not be amiss. She had lemon and chicken, but to cook would mean to leave his side. She was reluctant to do so as of yet. She pressed the cloth to his temples gently and he groaned softly in response.

A cold or a flu could kill as easily as venom. She prayed it was not that bad, and she was simply being overly emotional. It could be caused from travelling without enough water. He said the trip made him unwell, after all. It would not be out of line for the good doctor to forget to drink enough, or eat enough, while immersing himself in his work.

If that was the case, she should begin on the soup right away and draw up more water for him to drink. Eleanor placed the cloth in the bowl of water with a soft sigh. She could check on him periodically while waiting for the broth to brew.

That would have to do.

She checked the fireplace and stoked the low flames back to life before leaving his chambers, keeping the door cracked in case he called out for her. It was a long way from the bedrooms upstairs to the kitchen, but it was better than doing nothing. For an added measure, she placed a bell on his bedside table. At one time it was used to summon maids to the chamber. After her mother passed away, her father had been consumed with grief and sent all of the workers from the estate, leaving the two of them to the cold walls of the manor alone. Henceforth, it collected dust in their drawers. For it to have a use again was nice.

Even if he was too ill to speak, she was sure she would hear the bell from a mile away. It was heavy and only rusted slightly around the curve of the bell by the wooden handle. It was finely crafted to stand the test of time for generations of nobles and lords. Or professors who were far too absorbed in their work to be left unattended for long.

She kissed his warm forehead and slipped into the hall. While she was tending to her father's needs, someone needed to feed the Theridiidae before the day was over. She could do that after delivering his meal and calling for the local doctor if his condition turned worse.

A small brown spider was climbing up the edge of the clay bowl she had been using to tend to her father. She smiled as she watched the tiny creature test the surface of the rim before turning away and scurrying back onto the safety of the table. Carefully, she placed her hand in front of its path and waited as it cautiously climbed onto her palm. Curling her fingers to prevent it from escaping, she brought the spider up to her chest.

Yes, she could take care of them all.

Chapter Thirteen

Silas awoke to the soft glow of the fireplace lighting the room. His breathing was hard as he shook off the remains of a nightmare that he could barely remember. Something about demons laughing in the halls. He licked his dry lips and slowly pulled himself up against the stack of pillows on his bed.

Bed? How did he get here?

With a groan from the effort, he reached over to the small oak table that had a glass of water someone thoughtfully left for him. He drank it greedily, reeling in the cool contrast to his sore, dry throat. When the contents had been drained, he replaced the glass on the table and looked around the chambers.

Besides the fire, nothing else had been touched. He had been feeling tired and nauseous when he arrived from Mr. Meyers, but the rest was foggy.

His stomach still rolled, and his body felt weighted with lead, but he needed to check on Eleanor and get back to work. Hopefully the illness would pass quickly so he could return to his normal duties without being weighed down.

Eleanor…

His eyes widened as the fog started to lift over his mind. Panic made him jump from his bed, almost collapsing again as his weak legs were forced to suddenly bear weight. Righting himself, he stumbled to his door and threw it open.

"Eleanor!" He cried out.

She had been bitten by 9958 and he fainted instead of being there to contain the situation. Was she alive? Gods, she had to be. He could not live if his whole family was stolen from him.

"Eleanor!"

His body was ice cold as he peeked into her empty room. She could be stuck downstairs, suffering alone and it was his fault. How had the new specimen escaped? Gods, he was a horrible man. He must have left the lid askew in his rush to meet up with the board for his grant.

Moving as quickly as he could, he took the staircase two at a time. From the echoes of the empty halls he caught light humming, and the mouthwatering aroma of chicken soup. It slowed him down as he turned to the kitchen instead of the dining room.

It could not be…

But standing in front of a large black pot, with a stained apron tied neatly around her waist, was his beloved daughter. She bopped her head to the tune that she hummed while stirring dinner and checking a recipe book opened next to the stove. She paused, running a delicate finger down the worn page of the book with a small frown.

"We do not have any parsley…," she mumbled.

Once again, Silas felt faint. She was alive and appeared to be fine. Had he simply imagined the bite? Never had he been so happy to be wrong. His illness must be worse than he originally thought.

"Eleanor, my dear, that smells divine! But tell me, how are you feeling?"

She startled at his voice, dropping the ladle into the pot as she whirled around to face him. "Me? I am fine, Father, but how are you? Should you be moving so soon? You collapsed in the dining room…"

He waved off her concerns while leaning nonchalantly on a countertop. "I am alright, simply tired. That ride took more out of me than I expected it to," he reassured her.

She did not look convinced but nodded and turned back to her work. "Why do not you have a seat? The soup is almost done. I shall bring out your bowl shortly."

Silas pursed his lips but nodded in agreement. His legs still felt weak underneath him. "Very well, if you need any help please call."

She flashed him a smile. "Of course, Father. Now, go rest a little more."

He reluctantly left the kitchen and crossed the hall to their dining room where he took the head of the table as usual. It felt good to sit back, even if only for the moment. While lost in thought, Silas missed the soft bristles that clung to his pant leg and slowly moved upwards. It was only when the eight legs bent to scale his knee that he looked down at the sandy brown tarantula that had chosen him as a means to get up to the table.

Silas tilted his head, puzzled that the Chilean rose was outside of the laboratory and on his leg no less. Carefully, he offered his hand to the creature and waited patiently as it slowly climbed into his palm.

"Eleanor? Did you go into the lab today?" He called out.

Her head popped into the room. "Yes. They needed to be fed and you were unwell. Why do you ask?"

He held up the spider with a cocked brow. "I am afraid you allowed one to escape, my dear."

She covered her mouth as a dark blush swept across her cheeks. Her eyes were widened in horror as she rushed over with an empty glass for him to deposit their surprise guest.

"I swear, I followed all of the protocols. I do not know how this one could have slipped past my sights! I am so sorry, Father. I did not mean to let him out!"

He gave her a very stern look. "You need to be more vigilant when you're in my lab. This one is harmless, but it could have easily gotten lost inside our walls or wandered outside and died in the cold. This is my work, and these creatures rely on us to keep them safe. What would've happened if the black widow escaped? You cannot be so reckless!"

She bit her bottom lip and bowed her head. "I wanted to help you. Your fever was so high… And this has never happened before, Father. I promise I had not meant to let it out."

"I know, but we need more precautions in place now. We *cannot* have this repeated in the future."

She nodded as he stood up and slowly walked

to the hall.

"I am putting it back and rechecking your work. Please have my supper out by time I return."

"Of course, Father. I am sorry," she mumbled.

"I know, Eleanor. I shall be back shortly."

Chapter Fourteen

The jar was empty with the lid left on the desk by a roll of tape they used to mark and seal each container. It was odd. It may have been an accident if she was concerned about burning the soup, but it was such a sloppy mistake that Silas could hardly believe his daughter had done it. Unless it was not a mistake… Did she purposely leave the jar open for the tarantula to escape? Why would she do such a thing?

No, Eleanor would not sabotage their studies. She was as passionate about arachnids as he was. And she had a brilliant mind, much the same as his own. Something else must have happened. But what? It could not have been the Chilean rose. He studied the spider for months and it never demonstrated the strength to open the jar lid, much less move it across the room before scurrying up the steps and out of the door.

Silas reapplied the seal and straightened his vest. The incident sent shivers down his spine, but he could not explain it. Perhaps it was a simple oversight. Surely it would not happen again. That did not calm the eerie feeling that hung over him, though.

Too many coincidences were popping up around Muffet manor. Too many dark omens and visions plagued him to dismiss something such as a missing spider so quickly. Did he really hallucinate the spider bite? Or was Eleanor experiencing a toxic venom that was slowly stealing her mind?

He swallowed thickly and quickly marched over to the other iron door. As fast as he could, he unlocked and unlatched the door and stepped inside. The lamps still burned brightly, illuminating every corner of the small room. He walked up to specimen 9958 and examined the seal. Still there, untouched and beyond that was the faint tints of green legs near the glass of the jar.

Years of being a scientist had made him mad.

Shaking his head, Silas locked up and left the lab. When he reemerged in the dining room, his spot had been set as he had asked. The bowl of chicken soup still steamed with heat, and his glass had been filled with water. He smiled softly and took his seat, looking over at his daughter whose head was bowed.

"I am truly sorry," she murmured.

He sighed and closed his eyes before reaching out to place a comforting hand on her shoulder. "No harm done, Eleanor. It is taken care of." When she looked up at him with glossy eyes, Silas sat up straighter and motioned towards their dinner.

"So, let us eat! This looks magnificent as always, my dear."

She smiled and gingerly picked up her spoon. "I made it from mother's old recipes. I hope it helps chase the last of the illness from you."

He returned her smile. "You're very thoughtful. I am sure it will."

They ate in silence for a few moments, each taking the time to savor the rich flavors of the thick broth and tender bits of boiled chicken. Silas dipped his spoon back into the broth and inhaled deeply. Almost his stomach was settling, and his strength was returning. Until he looked into his bowl and saw a maggot floating with his rice and chicken. He blinked but was not mistaken about what he saw. Swallowing back bile, he looked over at his daughter who was eating without any concerns.

"Sweetheart, are you sure you followed the

recipe exactly as it said?"

Eleanor gave him a puzzled look but admitted she did not. "We were out of parsley," she explained.

"Ah, and did you substitute anything else for the parsley?" He asked with a forced gentle smile.

She raised a brow in suspicion but shook her head. "Does it taste that bad? I could try some other herbs to supplement it next time."

"No, no," Silas said quickly. "The seasoning is fine. Uh, it is just that. Well, you see…" He racked his brain to try and find a way to tell her about the parasite without insulting her cooking. So far, he was doing a terrible job with it.

Eleanor giggled as he floundered. "Eat up, father. You need your protein to regain your strength. If the seasoning is not bad, what's wrong with the soup?"

He opened his mouth, closed it, then simply pushed his bowl in her direction. "Sweetheart, I do believe we should have some rolls for dinner instead. It seems maggots somehow wound up in your cooking," he stated as gently as he could.

She peered into his bowl before slowly nodding. "As I said." She looked up at him with cold, dark eyes. "You need your protein."

Chapter Fifteen

"Father, are you alright? You're looking flushed again," Eleanor inquired with a frown.

"What did you say? Just a moment ago?" Silas asked harsher than he had meant.

Her frown deepened. "I said that is not a maggot. It is a piece of rice." She leaned closer to him, hand poised to take his temperature. "I would not add something that could make us sick to our dinner. Are you sure you're feeling well?"

He waved her hand away and pulled his bowl back, stirring the contents around and eyeing each spoonful suspiciously. "It is…" All rice and chicken. He reached for his glass of water and took a generous drink. "I am fine. I am fine. Merely more tired than I had thought. Maybe I should retire early tonight…"

The concern remained on her face even as

she leaned back in her chair and continued to eat her own soup. The silence thickened around them before Silas finally took another tentative bite. It tasted right. The texture was not off putting or alarming. He must have imagined it. Again. Truly he was going mad.

He adjusted the collar of his shirt, popping free the first two buttons as he reached for his water again. His throat was so dry, and the room had become too warm.

"I am sorry, Eleanor. I had not meant to accuse you of such a thing. I know you would not do anything to harm us," he apologized sincerely.

She nodded but kept her eye on him as he began to sweat again. She licked her lips and pushed her own bowl away. "Father, you are sick truly. I am sending for a doctor. I believe your fever may be back," She admonished.

"Nonsense, it is simply exhaustion from the ride into town and back," he huffed.

"But you're sweating and growing pale again…"

Silas stood up suddenly, cutting off her concerns. "I am retiring for the night. If you feel a doctor can do better than a good night's sleep and some water, then fine. Get one. But I am sure your worries are over nothing. I will see you in the morning. Good night, Eleanor," he stated before turning on his heel and marching into the hall.

Eleanor bit her bottom lip as she eyed his half-finished soup and drained glass of water. Perhaps he was right, and some sleep would ward the rest of this… whatever it was, away. A nagging feeling in her gut told her that was a lie. That things were only going to get worse if they went untreated.

What was she supposed to do?

She took the dirty dishes across to the kitchen to wash them, then paused and peered out at the pink sky. It was too late to send for a doctor. It would be dangerous to go riding by the light of the moon alone. She supposed that answered that, then. She would wait until morning and keep a careful eye on him until they could get proper help.

The creaking of a door caught her attention. Curiously, she left the dishes behind to follow the sound down the back hall. The door to the lab had been left cracked open. Was not her father supposed to be in bed? Why was he trying to work while in his current state?

She narrowed her eyes as she slipped in the door and closed it firmly behind her. That man was too stubborn for his own good!

Only when she got to the bottom of the stairs, the room was empty. She checked between every bookcase, desk, and box she could find but no one else stood in the room with her. Had her father forgotten to shut the door all the way when he came down earlier? They were becoming sloppy, and that was dangerous. She eyed the quarantine room, the only other place someone could be without her seeing them. Did he go in to perform experiments on 9958? Why, when it was getting so late?

She unlocked the door and heaved it open, peering inside another empty room, save for the spiders, of course. Nothing looked disturbed. All of the seals remained intact.

Was she coming down with the same fever her father had?

With a shake of her head, she left and went back up to the main floor of the manor. Perhaps it was time for her to turn in as well…

As she walked up the staircase, another creaking sound sent a shiver down her spine. The house was old and made some odd noises, but this was someone opening another door. She was being silly for being concerned. Her father must have made it to his chambers and was going to bed. But then why, when she stepped onto the top floor, was her bedroom door open and every other door on the floor closed? She never left her door open, it could blow out the fire she lit for the evening, so she did not freeze during the night.

Cautiously she approached her room and peered inside from around the hand carved door frame. Her father stood by her window with his hands clasped neatly behind his back. He seemed calm, almost as if he was simply admiring the view her room had to offer of the grounds behind the house. But his room had the same view…

"Father?" She called out, carefully stepping inside. "Is there something you needed?"

He turned to look at her with such sorrow in his eyes that it broke her heart in two.

"You are the spitting image of your mother, you know," he stated softly.

Eleanor cocked her head to the side but moved out of his way as he walked to the door. He did not look back as he bid her a good night and left.

She licked her lips and looked out the window that had his attention. The strong oak tree had nearly bare branches that waved slightly in the winds. A single spider's web, woven between two high branches, gleamed from the glow of the full moon stood out, but nothing more.

"Please, tell me you're a good omen of what's to come," she begged quietly. In answer to her prayers, a single common house spider slid down the outside of her windowpane from a strand of shiny, white web.

Chapter Sixteen

Silas used the low moon light to walk through the yard in the chilly late autumn air. Neighs and whinnies rendered the air from within the barn as he approached the doors. His hand hesitated, his eyes darting back to the manor. It was well into the night and the sun would be rising within a few short hours. However, he could not shake the worry that Eleanor was still awake and wandering around. How did it come to be that he would fear his own daughter?

Silas shook his head and opened the old pull door. The horses inside watched warily as he stepped into the warmth. He closed the door behind him, cringing as it squeaked in the old rushed wheels. Numbers one, two, and three let out cries of protest when he stepped a foot closer to their stalls. Each beast lashed out at an invisible force behind them, and to their sides. Thrashing and shaking their heads in distress.

His heart sunk as he watched the poor creatures waver on their hooves. With so much on the line right now, this sight was nearly the final nail in the coffin. Had the serum failed? It was so promising just days before. But then, everything was promising just days before…

His throat was dry, and his headache was only made worse by the loud animals surrounding him. Everything seemed to be falling around him. Science was making his small family mad. His illness was contributing to this insanity and dragging him down a hole he was not sure he could climb from.

The horses had received minimal amounts of the venom. Their suffering should have been reduced to trace levels. Yet here they acted as paranoid as he felt and were striking out with agony in their eyes. The antibodies grow inside of them. The venom should be gone.

How was this possible? How did 9958 do this much damage within a massive being? Why did he have no answers when he spent countless hours investigating this case? He was failing as a father and a researcher.

Silas clenched his fists and release a roar into the rafters. This had to change. He would not be beaten so easy! He was Doctor Silas Muffet. He would reclaim his family and research. No matter what.

***

The sun shone through the thin curtains that really needed to be replaced as Silas watched his daughter enter the lab with a frown. He was home, and the specimens had been fed so she had no need to wander down into his study. Yet she did, closing the door firmly behind her as if she was keeping him away from whatever it was, she was doing.

He hated to think his own beloved flesh and blood was capable of turning on him but the incident with the Chilean rose was too odd to forget so suddenly. He tucked his jacket around his body as a chill ran through him. The hot and cold flashes were getting worse. Not that he wanted to admit it out loud, but she may be right about him needing to see a doctor for his illness.

He waited patiently, hidden in a corridor off the side of the back hall for Eleanor to reemerge. The longer she stayed away, the worse his fears grew. She was becoming sloppy with the spiders, bordering on obsessed with the tender way she held them close to her heart while he fought in fever. Yes, he saw that, too. He saw the love in her eyes as she watched the common brown spider climb into her palm and then cradled it as if it were a child. It was not normal, even by their standards.

At first, he wondered if his work was too much, and had tainted her sanity. But then the fever overcame him, and he slid back into the abyss once more. Now that he was lucid, he wondered if her adoration for the arachnids was a part of the venom from 9958. He could not have imagined that.

While the spider appeared to be in the jar, he had no concept of how long it would take from the initial bite to her "recovery" from it to put the spider back. And as his daughter, she would make sure the spider was placed back in the lab before it completely escaped.

The new question was, why was not she dead yet? Darrell had succumbed to the toxin shortly after it was introduced—or so it was implied. What was different about Eleanor than Darrell that she still stood with almost no visible ill side effects? Or was she hiding them? More afraid for his health than her own.

Speculating did not do much but work him up into a panic. Cold or not, he needed to find a cure as quickly as possible to save his baby's life. But there, at the edge of the dim lanterns light, hopped a tiny thing no bigger than a dime. It was black with thin white stripes across its back, but extremely quick. Quick enough to have imagined? One moment it was there and the next it was gone. One blink and Silas would have missed its departure. Usually he considered spiders to be good omens but now... Now he questioned his beliefs.

When the lock turned, he spun around and made his way down the hall and upstairs. Yet, he could not bring himself to go to his own chambers. If he was being honest with himself for one moment, these may very well be his last minutes with his Little Miss Muffet.

He walked into her bedroom instead and did something he had not done in a very long time. He went to the window and prayed.

When she came in and caught him, he took a long moment to memorize her precious face with the high cheeks splattered with a light smattering of freckles his wife used to have. The long lashes that framed her jade eyes, always so wide and inquisitive. To the long blonde locks, she kept tied back from her face in braids or a neatly contained bun.

His whole world was standing before him.

Without her, there would be nothing.

He could not let that happen.

"Goodnight, Eleanor. I love you," he promised with a chaste kiss to her head.

Then he went to work.

Knowing that Eleanor would not approve of him working while suffering, he waited until the dead of the night to creep down into his lab and don his apron and gloves. His eyes were narrowed in determination as he unlocked the back-iron door and faced with 9958.

"If my daughter dies because of you, then you will exist no longer," he promised as he broke the seal to the jar and dumped the spider into the observation tank. First, he needed to acquire the venom in question, then he could work in reversing its effects. With so much on the line, he could not afford to make a single mistake. Time was precious and counting against him. He brought out a sample cup, only an inch tall with a leather piece banded around the top.

He needed 9958 to bite the taut leather and inject as much venom as possible into the cup to be used for analysis later. Luckily, the damned thing was so aggressive it would attack anything—or anyone—that came close to it. He only needed his tongs to hold her in place until the milking was finished.

Never before had a cure been developed in only a few short hours, but he was a determined man ready to break records. He levelled his gaze at the jeweled beast with his equipment right in his leather fists.

"I hope you're ready because I need you to give me enough venom to kill an elephant. Do not disappoint me, now. Bite!"

***

Silas worked until nearly dawn when his body could press on no further. His eyes stung and had become blurry from staring into the microscope. His hand cramped from jotting notes down as quickly as he thought of them. And his back ached from being hunched over for hours. His limbs were starting to shake as his collar grew hotter again. He groaned in pain.

"Not again, not so soon," he pleaded, but sweat was already beading his brow. Hours passed as if mere minutes and he was no closer to finding his cure than when he had started. Now, the clock chimed and demanded he pay for his perseverance when he was in no form to do so. It was inevitable. He must rest or he would collapse from exhaustion and be forced to sleep regardless.

Warily he removed his gloves and apron, leaving them at the desk with his scribbled notes and theories. His eyes moved over to the small vile of pain reliever he had concocted early on in the study. It didn't negate the true symptoms of 9958 as he had hoped, but this could be another use for it. His limbs were leaden and aching beyond anything he had felt before. If that pain could be lifted from his mind for a few mere moments, he could focus on the cure with refreshed eyes and gusto.

Silas filled a syringe with the serum then injected it into the crook of his arm. He hissed as the needle pierced his skin and emptied the dosage into his blood stream. He prayed it would take effect soon.

But exhaustion won out and after he replaced the needle on the desk, he turned away from his hard work. He climbed the worn staircase up to the manor. With any luck, Eleanor would still be in bed. Alive and fighting the horrid venom inside of her.

Muffet's were fighters. She would keep pushing back against the odds until the reaper claimed, "no more!"

He had time still. At least, that's what he had to believe.

Chapter Seventeen

The Zebra back spider was missing. Eleanor was sure she counted everyone else but the Salticus scenicus was not in his jar. The seal had been broken and the lid was left next to the container on the shelf, upside down as if someone had carelessly and hastily removed the top then dumped it to run. But why?

She fiddled with her apron as she eyed the rest of the lab. Her father's gloves and apron had been left on his desk with a pile of loose-leaf paper with intangible notes scrawled across them in half smeared ink.

Did her father accidentally leave the jar open? That would not be possible. He was meticulous in his work and took every precaution to contain the spiders that he could. But he was not feeling well and obviously, instead of resting as he should have, he came back to work while in a feverish state.

At least it was only one missing, and a rather common one at that. Still… She could not help but to wonder if he would blame her for it as he had with the tarantula. She never went near the Chilean rose yesterday, so she could not possibly have let it loose. Not even by mistake. And it was not possible for the spiders to simply undo their own lids and walk out.

This did it. She was going into town to get the doctor. He needed something to break his hallucinations and get him back to the brilliant man she knew, and the kind father she loved.

Something crashed from above and her heart jumped. She ran up the stairs to the parlor where her father had dropped a cup of tea. He was on his knees, picking up the pieces when he noticed her in the doorway staring at him. He offered her an unsteady smile and tossed the bits of broken glass into the small trash can by one of the plush, green chairs. The kettle remained on the long dark table with the saucer and sugar bowl. She sighed, leaving to grab a cloth before coming back to watch him rise slowly to his feet.

"I am afraid I lost my grip on the cup and it fell. Give me the towel, darling, I shall clean the mess up," Silas explained.

"No need, Father, I can do it. Did you want some more?"

He chuckled softly. "I do believe I have had enough sugar for the day, and you know I cannot have tea with only milk in it. No, I believe I should stay with water."

She knelt down on the floor by the small puddle and dabbed at the liquid. There was not much so he must have been almost done, anyway.

"We have some milk I could warm up for you," she offered, pitching another small sharp into the trash.

He shook his head and settled back into the chair. "I am fine, but thank you," he insisted.

Eleanor decided not to push any further and finished mopping up the floor. She stood and examined her work, tilting her head to be sure no tiny porcelain pieces were left behind.

It looked as if that had gotten everything, so she took the rag to the sink to be dealt with later, which reminded her of the dishes she forgotten about from the night before. Oh, dear, the chores were piling up again. But what could she do? She was one woman with an ailing father who needed her help more than the floors needed to be swept.

She returned to find him gone. She could only guess where he had gone and wondered if she really needed to track him down. With any luck, he ventured back to his chambers to lie down again.

If she left to fetch the doctor then she would be alone for a few hours. The thought was worrisome. What if he broke out into another high fever and collapsed? At least today he was looking a little better, even if he had not emerged from his room until noon. Should she go? Should she stay?

What about the missing spider?

She groaned at the thought of hunting it down and catching it again. They were quick, little jumpers. Heck, he may not even be in the house anymore.

Eleanor nibbled her bottom lip as a wicked voice reminded her the spider could be replaced. It was a relatively common thing, surely, she could capture another and place it into the jar with none the wiser. However, that was doing more than simply deceiving her father—something she entirely detested—it could compromise their study on it so far. No, replacing it was out of the question unless it was discussed at length with her father.

Who was ill.

And she was back to moral square one.

A soft click from down thc hall jolted her from her thoughts. He was back in the lab. But why?

Why was not he in bed so she could tend to his sickness? Almost angry at her bullheaded father, Eleanor spun around to march downstairs when a wave of dizziness overcame her. She gripped the counter tightly while swaying on her feet with one hand pressed to her forehead. It took a moment for the feeling to subside and after it did, she noted happily that her skin felt cool, not feverish. It would be devastating should they both come down with the same sickness.

Eleanor paused and slowly brought her hand down from her head. It was bare. Both of her hands were. What happened to her gloves? She never went a day without wearing a pair, so she must have donned some before wandering down to make breakfast. Or did she forget in her fret for her father's well-being?

She shook her head as she tried to remember dressing in the early rays of the morning. She could not recall much detail besides opening her closet to pick out a dusty rose dress.

"It is not important," she told herself as she stood up straight. She needed to go get her father into bed and fetch a doctor. He needed help. She would help him, even if she had to chain him to his own chambers to do so.

Chapter Eighteen

Time was of the essence. If Silas' theory was correct, then the initial bite Darrell had received was a few days prior to his ultimate demise. According to the letter from Professor Wilder, they first made contact with 9958 three days before attempting to capture it for study. It was hard to gauge when Eleanor was attacked. His own sickness stole precious seconds from him, and the fever could have made him hallucinate the first bite until he broke it. Assuming, however, that the fever did not play his mind against him, this was the third day and Eleanor's last sun set. Already the veins in her heart shaped face were standing out stark against her skin.

Silas felt his stomach turn and his hands shook as he moved the vial of venom extract to the side of his work station. He picked up his quill and jotted down another addition to his formula. The damned substance did not react as he had expected. It rejected nearly every adjuvant chemical he had introduced to it thus far.

The fates could not be so cruel as to steal his entire family away from him. That would be too great of a loss for him to endure.

The door to the lab rattled against its thick hinges. Silas swallowed hard and pushed back the guilt as he patted his pocket where Eleanor's key resided. He had no choice but to steal it while she tended to his mess. A mess he had made just for this moment. The venom needed his undivided attention and her refusal to allow him peace to continue the study required some tough choices. She would forgive him after she recovered her mind.

Three sharp bangs followed the rattling and Silas could have sworn he heard her angered screams of denial fill the house.

"Be patient my sweet little Miss Muffet, I shall find your cure soon. I promise. Give me a few more hours, that's all I ask," Silas tipped his head back to stare at the ceiling with tears pooling in his green eyes.

"And those in our Heavens above, I beg of you, do not take my daughter away from me."

When silence filled the chambers once more,

he took a deep breath and focused on his notes. Somewhere within the mess of formulas and theories was the answer to his prayers. He simply needed to find it. However, even if he discovered his mistake without a proper test of the drug, he could still have the dosage wrong. Typically, they used a lab rat, or even a rabbit to gauge how it would react to the serum first. Then they moved on to testing on humans. Silas was going to skip a vital part of the testing phase and that scared him as much as the thought of *not* discovering the cure did.

Out of frustration and brewing anger, he picked up a beaker of distilled water and threw it across the room where it shattered and splashed against the stone wall. Was this all for naught? It could not be. He was the great Doctor Silas, after all, he had saved hundreds of lives before. He needed to remember that as he turned back to his notes with a groan. The ink markings were beginning to turn into a foreign language. All of the equations looked the same.

His brows drew tight as he leaned closer to the paperwork. Wait! There! At some point Silas mixed up a 3 with an 8, completely changing his formula and ruining the measurements required to create the antidote. Sweat had collected on his forehead as he adjusted the equation and reached for the vial of venom again. His face paled as he stared at the three drops remaining. It would not be enough, but he feared that 9958 would soon stop cooperating with him as he milked it continuously to experiment with the drug. It could not be helped, he had to extract more whether the creature enjoyed it or not.

Silas unlocked the door to 9958's enclosure and prepped the quarantine tank. With his supplies at the ready, he turned to the sealed jar of his most despised projects. When this was over, he would have nothing to do with the spider ever again. It could be passed off to a different arachnologist. Quickly, he twisted the lid and unceremoniously dumped the spider into the tank from the top lid. Grabbing the long tongs and leather capped vial, he took a steadying breath and reached in for the jade creature.

"Do not be shy with me now. We need to do this one more time," he muttered as 9958 evaded the tongs and darted around the offered vial. "Give me one more bite."

With bated breath, Silas watched the cornered jeweled spider rear up, and then sink its fangs into the top of the vial. Slowly the dark venom dripped down the glass walls and collected. It only lasted a moment before 9958 released itself and scurried away, giving him a meager amount of venom to work with, but with any luck it would be enough.

"Stay here, I shall be back for you as soon as I finish the cure," the doctor promised as he closed the lid of the large tank. He eyed the spider suspiciously for a moment, then turned away and headed back out to the main room of the lab.

Chapter Nineteen

Eleanor tilted her head at the door of the lab. Father locked her out. She pitied him now, his delusions were obviously worse than she had thought. The poor man was suffering, and thought she was his enemy. It was heartbreaking.

If only she could make him see she had his best interests at heart. That she loved him so dearly she would do anything for him.

That's why when he refused to answer her calls to him, she turned away. Steel could not be cut away, but it could melt if the fire was hot enough. It was the perfect plan, the cellar spiders lining the hall told her so. Their long, thin legs reached out to her as though they recognized their mistress. Their mother. Their true, benevolent caretaker. She smiled at them in passing and turned to the kitchen where a small door to the pastures outside resided. They rarely locked it as most predators could not scale nor burrow beneath the face to the estate, and their closest neighbor lived a mile away.

The smooth iron handle turned silently in her grasp and the fresh air of the afternoon rushed in to greet her. It was simply lovely. The sun was high in the cloudless sky, with the few trees dancing as she passed them by. The stable doubled as a shed, housing many landscaping supplies inside with the hay and horses they needed for their cures, and to get into town. The barn smelled from the manure and the majestic animals inside, who were less than enthused to see her—such fickle beings.

It did not matter, what was important was the axe they kept propped up near the doors. The fireplaces needed to be restocked before she could appropriately retrieve her father. Eleanor picked up the tool and waved at the horses who stomped their feet and neighed in reply. Then she walked around the back to the pile of logs that had been gathered but not trimmed enough to use indoors.

Humming softly to herself, Eleanor placed a small log on top of the old tree stump with deep grooves from years of use on the top. The cold, bitter wind tore through the thin long sleeves of her gown, as she had forgotten to grab a proper jacket. It would only slow her down anyway, besides she barely felt the chill as she worked diligently on slicing apart the lumber.

This was cutting into precious time, but it needed to be done. Next time she would not be so careless with the chores. She would demand the same of her father after he recovered.

Eleanor widened her stance as she brought the axe up over her shoulder.

Yes, there would be some big changes in the Muffet manor. Changes for the better—she would see to that personally.

With as much strength as she could muster, Eleanor brought the sharp blade down and split another log in half. She dropped the weapon and added the pieces to a slow growing pile. Four turned into six, which turned into eight. "A few more and that should be enough for now," she mused as she placed another log on the tree stump. She would worry about the rest to warm their personal chambers later.

Axe up, and then down with a resounding *crack*! Her fingers were turning pink and for a moment she thought she saw thick, inky webs spreading through the back of her hands. The veins were throbbing, and the darkness was growing, slowly climbing into each of her delicate fingers. With a sharp gasp, Eleanor dropped the axe and stumbled a step back. She opened her hands up and stared at the numbed palms, but the veins were gone and all she saw was reddening flesh again.

Eleanor swallowed hard and shook her head. It must have been a trick of the light, or her own overactive imagination perking up from the exhaustion of chopping wood. The lies her father rambled about must have woven into her sub-consciousness and were coming out in a brief moment of weakness. It was ludicrous, of course. She had been careful around spiders since she could walk. One would never manage to bite her, much less a venomous one, without her realizing it.

Eleanor stepped back up to the tree stump and picked up another small log. Soon she could start the fire and save her father from himself. Then she would take a nice long bath and get a good night's sleep. That would fix everything.

Chapter Twenty

It was with shaking hands that Silas extracted the cure into a thin needle syringe.

Untested.

Rushed.

Silas could not feel relieved with the final product clutched in his sweaty hand with so many possibilities still lingering in the air. Doubt and fear stole his peace and plagued him even as hope continued to beat in his wary heart. What if he miscalculated another number? What if he had missed a critical step in his haste?

A headache pounded behind his eyes, drawing a groan from him as he shook the negative thoughts away. It would work. He was a brilliant scientist who maliciously recorded his work. Every ingredient was accounted for. Every step had been taken to ensure the best results when it was administered to his daughter. Eleanor would surely live. All he needed to do was coax her into allowing him to give it to her. Perhaps he could disguise it somehow? No, she was too smart to fall for such an easy trick.

Silas leaned back in his chair while mulling over his new dilemma when the sounds of creaking floorboards caught his attention. Fear slithered down his spine as those steps moved back and forth from one end of the house to the other. Back and forth. Back and forth. Each step carefully measured and as light as they could be. What was his daughter up to? And did he truly want to know as the hallucinations toyed with her once sharpened mind?

Silas quickly rose to his feet, but dizziness swept through him causing him to fall back into his chair until the room stopped spinning. He lifted a hand to his forehead, closing his eyes against the rising nausea. He overworked himself and was now paying the price for it. But it was worth it to see his beloved Miss Muffet safe once more. With renewed determination, he slowly stood again and made his way across the lab. The spiders watched him curiously as he walked past their shelves. Some tapped the glass with their long front legs but were ignored as he continued to the dimly lit steps.

A niggling feeling of foreboding brushed across his senses, making the fine hairs on his arm stand up. The closer he came to the door, the more he feared he would be too late. The soft glow of the light around him danced and flickered on the walls, making him blink twice as curls of smoke drifted in from beneath the thick locked door. He swallowed hard and grasped the iron handle, hissing softly as it burned in his hand. Silas threw all of his weight into the door and burst into the hallway, knocking something back in the process. That something let out a sharp gap before thumping on the floor a foot away. Fire was growing around the doorway, eating the wooden walls and licking at his stunned body.

Eleanor shook her head, looking up at him with a dazed expression and a burning torch inches from her sprawled out form. His instincts to protect his daughter outweighed his fear and anger over what she had done.

"Eleanor, move!" He barked as the flames steadily grew near her hand. He could not watch to see if she had listened, much as he would have preferred. Silas whipped off his coat to beat at the fire raging around him and stomped at the heat burning by his shoes. Sweat coated his brow as he soon gave up on his efforts to smother the flames and spun around to get to the kitchen to fill a bucket of water. Eleanor had listened and fled, leaving behind her ravenous mess. Good. He would yell at her later when they were both safe, and she was no longer under the effects of the poison pumping through her veins.

The bucket overfilled and sloshed on the ground as he hazardously jogged with it to the lab entrance. He threw the cold water on the flames, washing the ones licking at the top steps away. The ceiling was his biggest problem as half of the hall now burned with thick black smoke accumulating above his head. Another trip to the kitchen and Silas returned to soak the abandoned torch. It was getting harder to breath as he ran back and forth, drenching as much of his home as he could. He prayed the entire time, hoping that his efforts weren't in vain and the fire could be stopped before it killed anyone.

His breath came out in harsh pants and his muscles protested the next trip to refill the bucket. The water from the sink poured out too slow for his liking, but he got it filled and stumbled back out to the halls. His clothes were plastered to his body from sweat as he drowned the last of the hellish flames. The walls were charred but the damage looked superficial. Perhaps the Lord was looking down upon him after all.

Silas dropped the bucket and collapsed to his

knees, wheezing in the smoke that still lingered but unable to force his body to move. Relief was cold in his veins as he realized he was not too late. Eleanor was fine and running around somewhere within the manor.

It was not too late.

Chapter Twenty-One

Pain.

Why did she hurt so badly? An ache dug itself deep within her bones and her heart was being squeezed by an invisible force. Eleanor sat in the fetal position on the floor of the upstairs hallway, hugging her legs tightly to her burning chest. She could not remember how she had gotten here, but her mind was awash with guilt and horror.

And her throat. It felt raw and dry as the desert. A gallon of water would not be enough to quench the slaking thirst but oh! How she craved it all the same!

Slowly she began rocking back and forth as she attempted to force the memories of the last few hours back. Had she only lost an hour or two? How much time was missing from her?

"Why is this happenning?" She sobbed,

raising one trembling hand up to stare at the thick black veins pulsing under her skin. She was living a nightmare. Worse yet, her father was living the same horror as she.

A flash of memory overcame her. Her father's face strained with grief and stress as he yelled, "Eleanor, move!" While an inferno raged around him.

Eleanor clamped her eyes shut and rocked harder as she grasped at her temples. She gritted her teeth against the pounding in her head and tried to push that memory back. He looked so scared, angry, and disappointed in her. An acrid stench of smoke clung to her clothes making denial hard to sink into. It was real. It had happened. A fire burned and her father gazed down at her as if she was somehow related to it.

But what did she do?

As she erupted into tearless sobs, her body shook much as a willow tree would in the harsh spring winds. The need to run still courses through her veins, but her body refused to listen. She remained rocking on the floor while swallowing back the rising bile in her throat.

"Eleanor? Little Miss Muffet?" Her father's warm voice called out, soothing some of her frayed nerves.

"Daddy!" She sobbed back.

"Hang on, hunny, I am going to make it better," he promised as he rounded the corner of the staircase. His smile was soft as he took in her disheveled state. For a moment she felt safe. Secure. Her father would protect and care for her as he always had.

Then he stepped into the light and she could see the thick black lines under the skin in his face. His warm grey eyes turned orange as she slowly prowled towards her. Those bright, straight teeth sharpened into long canines dripping with saliva, eager to tear into her flesh.

"No, no, no," she whimpered in horror. Her mind was betraying her. It was casting illusions and making her ill . But the monster standing before her was real, drawing a long syringe from its pocket out. And it was going to kill her.

"Do not worry, baby, this will only hurt for a moment. Then everything will be alright," it garbled with a wicked grin.

"Eleanor, move!"

She tripped over her own feet in her haste to flee, nearly tumbling back to the cold, wooden floor. Righting herself took two seconds too many, the creatures callused fingers brushing over the edges of her skirts. With a stifled sob, Eleanor grabbed the front of her skirt, held it high, and managed to escape the monster's grasp. She ran down the hallway with a darting glance to each empty room she passed. Her mind was whirling at breakneck speed, attempting to form a plan. Unfortunately, her odds did not appear to be in her favor. Most of the rooms upstairs did not lock, nor did they offer a way to flee outside without risking a broken bone or two in the process. Perhaps a barricade would work?

Eleanor bit her bottom lip while daring to look behind her. The monster impersonating her father was only a few feet back, but the end of the hallway was drawing near. She did not have a choice; she would have to try it and pray that God smiled down on her.

Eleanor ducked into a spare bedroom on her left, quickly slamming the door behind her. Her breath came out quick and choppy as she scoured the room for something large enough to delay her pursuer, yet light enough that she could move on her own. What luck! A long, mahogany desk covered in a thin layer of dust stood two feet from her left. The top was bare of knick-knacks or pens with a single matching chair pushed in tightly. At one point this piece of furniture would have been stunning in the low light of the setting sun, but now it was a reminder of the barren estate that stretched across the massive grounds. It would not be easy to move, but she did not need to push it very far.

Eleanor ripped the chair away and pressed herself against the far edge of the desk. With her eyes trained on the door, she threw all of her weight into the desk and slowly inched it across the floor. Sweat gathered at her brow as pain lanced through her side, thrusted into the unforgiving mahogany. Her shoulders and arms protested the horrid journey merely a few feet forward. Every second ticked ominously by in silent, save for the scratching of the desk legs against the floorboards.

Once she had the desk in place, she let out a sigh of relief and allowed herself a moment to regain her breath. It was hard not to wonder how she managed such a feat without being intercepted by the beast outside. Surely it would have caught up to her by now? Or even minutes ago when she began to push the monstrous desk against the door?

Eleanor swallowed hard and nervously patted her skirts. The door did not rattle with an attempt to break in. No footsteps could be heard travelling through the halls. It was far too quiet to be safe.

What happened? Where was the creature stalking her? Had she truly escaped?

Doubtful. But this gift would not be wasted. In these moments of peace, she would find her freedom and then save her real father.

Chapter Twenty-Two

Silas watched his daughter dart into one of the spare rooms with his brows knitted together. At first it appeared she was relieved to see him, but something had changed. Was the venom tricking her into believing he would hurt her? His heart dropped as a loud scraping sound echoed down the hallway. His poor little Miss Muffet. She was suffering and he was no closer to helping her. He needed a new plan.

Silas turned on his heel and startled at the sight of a Brazilian White knee Tarantula standing in the middle of the floor. The creature was harmless, with a body size of around 3 inches long. The legs had bright white bands around the joints that glowed in contrast to the fine black hairs covering the rest of its body. But how did it escape the confines of its case?

Silas shook his head and tucked the syringe back in his pocket. It was a mystery as was every other escape so far. And as much as he would prefer to tuck the sweet specimen back in the proper jar, he had more pressing matters to deal with. So, for the first time in his life, he ignored the spider and continued down the hall.

Presumably that loud scraping sound was Eleanor blocking the door, meaning he would need to find a new way to get to her. At this point was hard to accept that brute force would be necessary to administer the anti-venom. The thought disturbed the professor as he had never so much as hugged his daughter too tightly before. But for her own good, he would do what needed to be done.

Silas travelled down the staircase briskly, only pausing to grab his warm wool coat from the front hanger, before pushing open the front door and stepping out in the bitter autumn winds. He buttoned the jacket as quickly as possible while maintaining his stride around the side of the house. The plan would be to scale the side of the house up to the room she was holed up inside of. How he was going to manage that was something else entirely.

They kept a ladder in the stables, but the ladder was not long enough to stretch up a story to her room. And while he was fit for a man his age, he did not exercise more than long walks on a warm day. Climbing the rest of the way up the house would be impossible without some sort of aid. Silas frowned to himself as he pondered his predicament. Thankfully this meant Eleanor could not leave, either, without risking grave injury to herself. Silas swallowed, hoping that thought would be enough of a deterrent to her that she would not dare try to jump.

Fear made man do the insane without a second thought.

Silas counted every window he passed at the back of the house, careful with his step to avoid rabbit burrows and protruding rocks. He could see a curtain fall back into place near the end of the building and almost smiled. Eleanor surely realized she could not escape from that high up and was probably searching the room for another means to flee. Luckily, there were none. Least, of course, she shoved whatever piece of furniture blocked the door away. He supposed that would be her next course of action, and it would make things decidedly harder on himself.

A wave of fatigue washed over his body, making his limbs heavy and weak. Already this day was taking its toll on him. Silas forced himself forward and stood underneath the window of her temporary prison. He could rest after she was safe.

Silas tilted his head, eyeing the sloped roof below the window sill. If the wind stopped for a moment, and he had perfect balance, he could scale the roof to enter the window. Or slide off of the roof and land in a heap on the ground. It was not a perfect plan, but it was the best he had come up with so far. With a deep breath of determination, Silas spun around and set forth to the stables to grab the ladder.

It was after the item in question was propped against the side of the manor that Silas realized this may be the most foolish thing he had ever done. There was no guarantee at this point that Eleanor remained in her chambers and his attempts may be for naught. Then there was the danger of scaling a roof that had not seen any work on it in years to consider…

After this matter was resolved, he promised to put some work into the estate. It needed touching up and had been neglected for far too long. Pushing the negativity aside, Silas grasped the sides of the wooden ladder and began his ascent to the window sill. His eyes were kept trained in front of him as his heart kicked up a notch the higher he climbed. The wind was still blowing enough to shake the rungs his feet rested upon, and for a moment he truly wanted to climb back down to safety and think about another way inside. Maybe he would find something big enough to break the door in. However, that was a slim chance indeed, or at least not one he would be able to hold much less swing around.

Steeling his nerves, he pressed on until his hands grasped the top rung on the ladder and his eyes were focused on the sloping roof with a handful of missing tiles. Silas licked his lips and reached out with his right hand to grab the edge of the roof, testing its ability to hold his weight as he pushed himself upwards. It seemed to hold well enough, which did put some of his growing anxiety to rest. Flexing his hands to make sure their grip was tight on the ledge, Silas stepped up onto the top rung, then pulled himself on the roof. It was hard, his fingers scrambling to find purchase on the smooth surface of the tiles as he tried to wrestle the rest of his body up. His legs kicked out against the wind while he stretched and inwardly screamed until he finally grasped the edge of a cracking tile and wrestled his body onto the roof. The tile broke afterwards but he thanked it for lasting as long as it did. With solid surface underneath his belly, he carefully pushed himself closer to the window sill with the strength of his toes and little help from his knees. He did not dare move too quickly for fear of losing what grip he had and falling down the dry grass below.

Success was short lived when finally, his fingers curled around the stone of the sill and he pulled himself close enough to peer inside at the lace curtains. The window was not locked, thankfully, but he could not see any moving shadows from within. Not wanting to lose hope, Silas quietly and slowly pulled the glass panel out and shifted up over the edge. The curtains fluttered in the breeze to give him a quick glimpse inside that sent his heart soaring. A long, heavy desk was still pushed against the door of the bedroom. He still had her!

Silas swung his leg over the edge of the windowsill and pulled himself inside when the soft whistle of the falling object touched his ears. Then, his body pitched forward, and everything went black.

Chapter Twenty-Three

Eleanor sat on the dusty bedspread of the old four poster in the center of the room. She smiled out at the sea of black arachnids that surrounded her as she plucked idly at the loose strings of the quilt. The shuffling outside was hard to miss and amused her almost as much as her subjects did. Did the beast think itself stealthy? Or was its arrogance so great it did not fear her when she had an army amassed to protect herself?

Venomous western black widows, redbacks, katipos, and funnel-web spiders climbed over one another as they stomped their tiny feet in eager anticipation. The window finally swung out and the curtains fluttered in the breeze. For a moment, she was staring at her father who was clumsily lifting his leg over the window sill. For a moment, her heart began to beat faster and the words to call off her army raced up to her lips. Then the beast fell inside, growling as his body met the unforgiving hardwood floors, and that moment was gone.

Softly she began to hum, plucking the strings on the blanket underneath her once again as the spiders swarmed together to face their prey.

"Dear God," the creature whimpered before scrambling up to its feet and backing away from the mass of legs and fangs. Those grey, panicked eyes searched her out and she met the beast's fear with a cool smile of victory.

"You forgot to ask if they were intelligent," Eleanor stated as her swarm stomped their feet in delight. The creature tilted his head in confusion, eyeing the room for an escape.

"Welcome home," she giggled. "Aren't you proud of yourself for finding a way inside?"

"Stop this insanity right now, Eleanor!" It demanded in a voice eerily close to her father's. Only the soft hiss at the end of its words gave the demon away. The illusions it could cast was impressive, if not for the severity of its crimes. How wonderful would it be to study this thing as she studied spiders? She could lock it away in a giant jar and test its ability to kill prey with large squirming snacks. It would be an incredible discovery within the scientific field—one that would surely put her on the map and force the world to see women as capable as men in science and math.

Eleanor sighed, what a dream but sadly, it was only that. She needed to kill this creature to end the nightmare plaguing Muffet Manor. She needed to find her real father and save them from the evil that had tainted their own walls.

The beast shook its head and closed its eyes while chanting, "this is not real." Under its breath.

Eleanor cocked her head and waved a brown recluse closer so she could run a single finger down the back of its warm body.

"Not real? That's an odd way to face your end. You cannot simply wish a wish and make reality float away. Life doesn't respond to whims and shooting stars," she mused.

The creature opened its eyes to glare at her and took a daring step forward. A mass of black widows piled over his feet and began climbing its legs. "You're right, which is why this nonsense will go on no longer! You're delusional, Eleanor. You were bitten by specimen 9958 and the venom is playing tricks on your mind!" It pleaded.

Eleanor shook her head and stroked the brown recluse again. "You're wrong. I was not bitten by anything."

"Really?" The beast scoffed as he pointed

to a vanity mirror across the room. "Then why is your skin ghostly white and your veins standing stark against your flesh?"

Eleanor did not want to look at his lies but her own eyes betrayed her and peered into the cloudy mirror. Her face looked shallow with thick black lines crawling down from her hairline to her eyebrows. Those same lines wove through her cheeks to her nose, and down her chin to her chest. Eleanor raised her hands and stared at her palms which had the same black, pulsing veins stretching to her fingers and wrists.

"No, I was not bit. I was not bit," she repeated, her voice kicking up an octave as her hands began to sweat. "There is nothing wrong with me!"

"Yes, there is!" The creature roared back, shaking the foundation of the house. Its hands clenched into fists as it took yet another step closer to her, all but ignoring the spiders swarming its body. How could it ignore the bites that pierced its flesh? The incisors dripping with venom and hatred...

Eleanor shook her head and crawled back an inch. "No, no, it cannot be true. I was not bit! My father was!"

The creature smiled sadly, withdrawing a long needle from its coat pocket. It looked down at the clear liquid filling the glass tube and tilted its head in thought.

"I know, baby," Silas cooed. "But I only made enough anti-venom for one of us."

Her father grabbed her foot and yanked her halfway off of the bed, causing her skirts to bunch up her mid-thigh. He jabbed the needle into her exposed skin and as she howled in pain, pushed down the plunger, injecting ice into her veins. Her howl became a scream as her body spasmed and lashed out on its own accord. Her eyes rolled back as her body filled with an agony she had never felt before.

"It is going to be okay, baby, I promise. I promise everything is going to be alright." She heard distantly as the walls slowly folded in on themselves. Faintly she registered a warm hand brushing across her forehead while the torrents of screams continued pouring from her parted lips. Her throat felt dry and scratchy, but she could not stop. Not until finally the last rays of the setting sun disappeared and everything went dark.

"I love you, my little Miss Muffet, never forget that."

***

Silas collapsed onto the bed next to his daughter as she whimpered in her sleep. He lifted a shaky hand and brushed the hair away from her eyes, pausing to examine the black veins in his own skin. Why had the venom affected them differently? Why was he able to see through the hallucinations when she could not? His strength was waning with each passing second. Simply sitting on the bedspread was hard to do in his weakened state.

Was this truly the end then?

Carefully he laid himself down, keeping enough space between them that should he accidentally lash out during the final throes he would not harm her in the process. Eleanor's features smoothed over, lit up only by the few candles struck on the bedside table. She was beautiful. A remarkable copy of her own mother. His eyes stung as he swallowed past the lump in his throat. She would have been proud of Eleanor, who did everything she could to beat every obstacle stood in her way. She was independent, brilliant, and loving. He was proud of her and wished he had the voice to tell her that one last time.

His eyes grew heavy as watched his daughter mumble incoherently in her sleep. He wished he could wish reality away and give them a few hours longer. However, Eleanor was right, life did not work that way. It had not when his wife past away, and it would not now. That did not stop him from closing his eyes and wishing anyway. And it was during that wish that everything slipped away from him and the pain he had been suppressing came forth to claim his body.

At least if he were to go, he could go, knowing his daughter was safe and alive.

And really, that was all a parent truly wanted—for their children to be safe, and for them to live as long as possible surrounded by happiness.

Eleanor would find hers again. She was a clever girl with the world at her fingertips.

Everything would be fine.

Chapter Twenty-Four

Eleanor awoke to the flickering of the waning candle with her body aching, and mouth filled with cotton. Her vision was blurry, and her mind was slowly taking stock of her surroundings. She felt as though she had been hit by a carriage, but physically was fine other than the needle protruding from her skin and the large dark bruise surrounding it. She swallowed hard, trying to chase some of the dryness away as she reached down with a shaking hand to remove the syringe and bring it closer to her eyes to examine. The long needle was stained with her blood, holding a drop of anti-venom at its very fine tip.

A shallow intake of breath forced her attention away and to the body next to her own. Silas laid on his back, his face pinched in pain and as pale as the moon. Dark circles encased his sunken eyes and sweat had beaded along his brow. His sacrifice came back to her and stung at her eyes. She swallowed again, clutching the syringe tighter as she drew it up to the waning light of the melted candles nearby. He injected her with the only cure he had created. He saved her at the cost of his own life.

But it was his own illusions that may have given him a second chance. For inside the syringe was half of the anti-venom still sloshing against the glass vial as she brought it closer to her unbelieving eyes. He had pushed the plunger down, but only half way. He administered enough of the medication to break through the worst of the venom. Now, she could use the last remains to save him before his last breath left, and together that could create a second dose.

Moving her body was hard, it was numbed and protested against her will to sit up. Eleanor gritted her teeth and forced herself closer to her father where she then rolled up his sleeve. Her hands shook as she carefully placed the needle against a thick vein in his forearm, then pushed it in until the tip was buried by his flesh. She pressed the plunger down as hard as she could, keeping it pressed down to be sure the last of the medicine entered his body.

Even after the vial was empty and his body

began to seize, she held the needle in so that not a drop would be wasted. His lips parted with a heartbreaking scream and his eyes flew open to stare at her in panic. Eleanor forced down the guilt that threatened to overtake her and held his body down the best that she could as he thrashed and shook.

Thick, hot tears rolled down her cheeks as she watched her father suffer. It was what had to be done, but that did not make watching the effects of the serum any easier. Is this what he had to endure when she was given the first portion of the medicine? Her father was strong… Even though she loved him more than anything else, Eleanor could not resist closing her eyes and trying to push the sounds of his suffering out of her mind.

An eternity too long passed before her father finally sunk into a restless slumber. Eleanor waited several more heartbeats before daring to peek at the man's prone form. His brows were still pinched in silent pain, but blessed silence enveloped the room. The candle light flickered and grew dimmer as the wax neared its end. She swallowed hard and swiped a hand over her tear stained cheeks. She should go and fetch another candle, just in case her father woke up while it was still dark out. She should but… Her body still felt heavy and sore. The thought of moving more than an inch made her internally cringe.

In a minute, she promised herself as she lay back on the mattress. The shadows danced across the ceiling as the flame struggled to stay lit. Outside, storm clouds gathered in the sky, blocking out the halo of the full moon. Somewhere in the distance, thunder crashed and rumbled. The weather seemed fitting for the moment, Eleanor thought distantly as she watched the room slowly dim. Darker. Darker. The shadows were barely distinguishable now.

She blinked as her eyes grew heavier. *Merely one more minute, and then I shall get up.* The bodies above her twisted and reached their long arms out to the far corners of the room. They moved to a beat she could not hear. It was entrancing. So fluid and beautiful.

Did the serum actually work, Eleanor wondered distantly. Was she still hallucinating, or was this something more?

Silas groaned and with some effort she turned her head to look over at him. His eyes were still closed, and she envied him for a moment. Sleep would be lovely, but she needed to get a fresh candle. The light flickered again, then went out as Eleanor blinked. She waited too long. Now it would be hard to navigate the hall to the closet for another candle.

The dancing shadows abandoned her as well. She imagined they were chased off by another clap of thunder outside. It was rather rude of the sky to interrupt their dance. She wanted to watch more. She wanted to see her father awake and smiling. She wanted…

She needed…

Eleanor yawned and could not remember. Her mind fled with the shadows and when she blinked again. She did not open her eyes back up.

Sweet blissful sleep captivated her and did not relent its enchanting hold until dawn.

***

Eleanor groaned as she leaned back in the old wooden chair at her father's work station. The numbers were beginning to blur together. The serum was nearly done, it only needed a few more ingredients and it would be complete. Time was still their enemy. She had left her father sleeping in the bedroom upstairs a few hours ago to pour over his notes. Her body was still sore from the battle with the venom from 9958. The spider in question was tucked away in her jar, agitated from when Eleanor pulled her out to milk her again. The process was quick. 9958 struck the taut leather top to the collection bottle without any hesitation. Eleanor was grateful for her cooperation. She was not sure she had the energy to fight with the tiny beast. Although she would have if need be.

Eleanor leaned back over the paperwork, worrying her bottom lip as she set the serum aside to recalculate the dosing. It had to be perfect or else they would risk overdosing on the medication. Granted, it would not be nearly as deadly as the venom was, but it would still wreak havoc on their recovering immune systems.

Vaguely she considered they would need to take stock of the arachnids still in the house. During their hallucinations a few of the spiders had been released. Finding them would be nearly impossible—if they were even still inside the manor. They could replace some of the more common species without much concern. The exotics would be a headache…

Eleanor rubbed her forehead before reaching over for the bottle of alcohol and a clean rag. She carefully disinfected a new needle while making a small mental adjustment to her father's notes. His work was brilliant, as she expected. For being under as much stress as he was, the formula was near perfect. It simply needed to be tweaked to accommodate for two separate doses. If she weakened the original and then lowered the amount administered, it would, in theory, eradicate the last of the venom's effect without putting either patient in danger. In theory. Nothing was proven until tested and that part made her hand waver as she drew out the serum into the clean needle's chamber.

Perhaps if she was quick enough, she could give it to her father while he continued to sleep. At least then, if she were wrong, he would not feel it. Eleanor swallowed against the sudden rise of bile in her throat. That was a horrible way to think! She needed to have more faith in herself, and in her father's research. If it worked once, surely it would work again.

Slowly she rose from her chair and turned towards the door. Everything seemed to pause as she drew in a steady breath. Yes, everything would be fine. Her father had said so himself. This would work. Eleanor took the first step towards the door with a little more confidence. Together they would see the next day.

Chapter Twenty-Five

"Eleanor?" Silas squinted, bringing a hand up to rub his forehead in confusion. He felt awful, as if his body was working to recover from a nasty illness. His stomach protested the thought of the water his daughter offered him from a fresh glass with condensation lazily trailing down the sides.

"No thank you, but…" His thoughts trailed off as he took in the brightly lit room. The sun was still high in the sky, indicating it was sometime in the afternoon. Was this simply a dream? Did he somehow survive the night? His head throbbed to remind him he was awake. Another groan escaped him as he attempted to sit up.

"What happened?"

Eleanor offered him a small smile while she placed the cup on the bedside stand and folded her hands in her lap. "You began to hallucinate shortly before you injected me with the serum. Or mayhap you were hallucinating sooner than that, I cannot be sure. But you failed to inject the full dosing, so I used what was left to stave off the venom in your body until I was able to prepare a new batch." She paused for a moment, worrying her bottom lip. "I dare say it worked. I do not feel any of the effects of the venom left in me. However, I could be wrong. We should test it as soon as possible."

He nodded slowly, taking in her information as he looked around the room. No spiders. No cobwebs. No mysterious demons hiding around the corners. He felt heavy and sore, but no worse for wear.

"How long has it been?"

Eleanor shrugged her delicate shoulders and played with a loose string on the quilt underneath of them. "It is only the day after. You had not slipped into a coma," she lightly teased.

Silas chuckled. "Well that is good. And what about the estate? Have you looked around to see what extent of destruction had been done?"

"The door around the laboratory is burnt, but it seems to be mainly superficial damage. I have not counted the specimens yet," she admitted, her brows creasing with worry as he pushed himself onto his feet. "Father, should you be moving so soon? I was not steady when I first awoke from the serum."

He waved off her concern but faltered with his first step, catching himself on the edge of the bed before his knees connected with the wooden flooring. "I shall be fine," he gritted out, waving her away again when she attempted to help him stand.

It took a few tries and couple soft growls but finally, he stood straight again and made it across the room to the door. "We should hurry, Eleanor. We need to make sure the other venomous creatures are still locked away, and that this nightmare is finally over."

Eleanor nodded and followed him down the hall. The stairs were easier, Silas could lean heavily on the railing to make his descent. The subtle scent of burning wood still filled the main floor. It would be a few days before the stench was completely gone. If only the weather was not so cold, they could then air out the house for a few hours.

They rounded the corner and Silas saw what his daughter had referred to earlier. The wallpaper was charred around the thick metal door of the laboratory. It curled and peeled away from the wooden walls. Soot covered the floor in a fine powder about five feet from where the fire had originated, and the trim around the door had large portions of it missing. The metal looked warped around the latch, but it did not ruin the lock.

His key slid into the hole and turned easily. The lock clicked open and they tugged the thick door open together. Inside everything was fine. The lamps still burned to light the way down the old staircase.

"Was the equipment alright?" Silas asked as they travelled down into the lab.

"I had dropped an empty beaker earlier, but the mess was swept up. That was the only thing damaged down here that I could tell," she admitted.

Silas nodded and automatically reached for his apron as soon as they stepped away from the stairwell. Eleanor followed his lead, donning a pair of thick leather gloves.

Silas took in the room quietly for a moment. Nothing appeared out of place. Perhaps it would not be as bad as he had originally thought. He turned to his daughter and smiled. "Shall we begin? Please grab some paper, I want everything recorded to review later."

Eleanor nodded. "Of course, Father. Though, this may take a while."

Silas grimaced as he surveyed the large room. "Then we had better get going. I want to be done by nightfall."

They started with the left side of the room, moving from shelf to shelf surveying each container carefully. The larger specimens were easy to find, but the web weavers were hidden in the depths of their thick webs. Eleanor took note as Silas had asked, careful to list the spiders they had found on a separate page than the ones who were missing. And much to his dismay, Silas found a few empty jars along the way.

"The Argyrodes argentatus is here," he announced while placing the jar sporting a striking yellow and black spider inside back onto the shelf.

"I found the Nephila pilipes," Eleanor added, peering into a tall glass jar with a few sticks placed in for the spider to spin its web off of.

"And here is the Tetragnatha montana."

Eleanor nodded and as she made a quick note of it in the leather-bound journal.

"That makes 53 spiders accounted for, with three known spiders missing. We still have the Salticidae to check, as well as the venomous ones." She stated, pointing to the locked door at the other end of the laboratory.

Silas nodded. "We're making great progress, but I fear it is already night. Perhaps we should split up to check the rest of the specimens.

Otherwise we may not finish until dawn."

Eleanor nodded and readjusted the journal in her arm. "That sounds fine with me. Which group did you want to examine?"

Silas frowned as mulled it over. As much as he wanted to keep his daughter under his protective wing, it would be faster if he looked through the jumping spiders himself. He was more familiar with them than Eleanor was. He would notice right away if one was missing.

"You go ahead and check on the venomous spiders. But please, do not open any of the jars!" He insisted with a pointed look.

Eleanor blushed. "Of course, Father. I shall be quick and careful."

Silas watched his daughter hurry across the room to the foreboding door. Worry gnawed at his stomach, but he could not linger over it. He trusted his daughter to take the proper precautions while inside of the venomous room. He only hoped everything was still taped up, and nothing was hiding in the corners of the room, waiting for the opportunity to strike.

Chapter Twenty-Six

Eleanor pulled the heavy door open and peeked inside. The room was dim, but nothing seemed out of the ordinary. Or at least, not that she could tell from outside. Cautiously, she entered the room and allowed the door to click shut behind her. The room felt as if it had shrunk, and the walls were pressing in on her. She swallowed and readjusted the journal in her arms. It was a trick of her mind, playing off the stress she was still under.

The jars sat on shelves carved into the stone walls. Each one had an innocent quality that belied the beasts inside. Of course, now she had nothing to fear. Should one of the arachnids be missing, they had the anti-venoms ready to combat them. As long as the spiders stayed within the house, anyway. If they had escaped outside… It could cause a catastrophe the world was not ready for.

Starting to her right, Eleanor peered inside a large square shaped jar containing a Brazilian Wandering Spider. It was once thought to be the deadliest spider in the world, and when they had received it to study, they were elated. Now, Eleanor had to wonder if 9958 was of more concern. The spider in question stepped closer to the front of its enclosure, the red fangs catching the flicker of the light. The rest of its body was a dark brown, almost bordering on black. It was rather large, similar to a North American Wolf spider. Her father had placed an empty coconut shell inside of the jar for the spider to sleep inside of. Even while tucked inside, it was easy to see the thick legs of the arachnid curled up for bed.

Eleanor took a moment to jot down the name before turning to the next specimen. The Sydney Funnel Web spider was one that they rarely interacted with. It was highly aggressive, even for a venomous spider, and could strike a victim multiple times with its large fangs before being satisfied and running away. They had yet to create a well working anti-venom on this one, but still worked diligently to procure it. Unfortunately, most of their test rabbits died within fifteen to twenty minutes of being bitten—making time of the essence to deliver a cure. They worried that even if they developed one, it would be of little use to children who were attacked.

The jar was still taped up, safe and secure. Of course, this spider, while dangerous to mess with, had never given them the problems that specimen 9958 had. Eleanor sighed and turned to the creature in question. The jar was unassuming on the wooden shelf, alone with a long shadow casted off from the low lighting. Thick webs filled every inch inside of the glass container, looking as innocent and undisturbed as a lazy cloud in the sky. Or perhaps it was closer to the cotton candy sold at fairs. Light and fluffy but incredibly hard to see through. The only reassurance Eleanor had was the tape still crossed over the metal lid.

She narrowed her eyes at the jar and approached it cautiously. It was hard to believe this tiny beast caused her and her father to face horrors they had never imagined before. The bite not only placed them near death's door; but turned them against one another and tested their bonds as nothing else could. To think there were countless others of its kind crawling around in the rainforest, making victims out of innocent men, women, and children… If there was a god, then specimen 9958 was created by the devil.

Eleanor grabbed a torch from the wall and

lifted the flames closer to the glass cage. A vague shadow appeared deep from within the cast of webs. Small, and resting at the bottom of the jar with its legs tucked close to its body. Without a doubt the spider was still contained inside of it is enclosure, no more a risk than any of the other venomous arachnids within the room. A sigh of relief escaped her, but a sliver of concern still clung to the edges of her mind. Were they truly done with the nightmare? So long as the creature remained, they would face the uncertainty of revisiting these past events every day from here on out.

An image filled her mind with a longing sense of temptation. She could simply knock the jar off of the shelf. Spiders were rather fragile creatures with an easy to crack exoskeleton. Any trauma to the cephalothorax would kill them instantly. It would be so easy to claim the act was an accident and stepping on the glass shards scattered on the ground was merely from her panic and horror at what she had done. Then the nightmare would truly be over.

Eleanor caught herself leaning closer to the shelf and stopped herself. She shook her head, banishing the thoughts away. They were researchers, facing death came with the job. She needed to accept that and stop blaming the spider for their struggles. It was due to their own negligence they had been bitten in the first place. That would be fixed with better procedures and safe guards in place for future studies.

She replaced the torch within its metal holder and gave the specimen one last look before turning towards the door. Everything was over now. They would take their time to recover and then begin their studies again with a fresh mind. Eleanor stepped out of the room and let the door swing shut behind her.

"Father, everything is fine in this room," she called out.

"Did you check to make sure each jar was closed tightly?" Silas called back.

"Of course, everything is still sealed and safe," Eleanor reassured him.

"Good, then let us finish this up and turn in for the night. I am exhausted."

As the lock clicked into place, silence filled the air. The lanterns flickered and dimmed as their oil ran low. The long shadow cast along the walls from the jars danced and moved. From one shadow in particular, a being separated from its containment. The long-jeweled legs sparkled in the orange hues of the flames. Slowly, ever so slowly, 9958 stepped out from behind the jar and wandered over to the edge of the shelf.

She clicked her mandibles together while running one thin leg over the smooth polish wood beneath her. The voices would be gone for quite a while, as usual, giving her plenty of time to spin her webs.

The humans should check on their pets more than twice a day.

The nightmare was not over yet…

Author's Note

All good ideas come at night, when you're overtired and willing to accept the possibility of almost anything. At least, it does for me. Around 3am I was at work and dreaming about writing my own fairy tale retelling. I had mulled over different stories that I enjoyed growing up, and how I could try to captivate the audience with a fresh look at the concept. The only problem that I came across was my inability to conceive something that hadn't been done before.

After seeing all the retellings of classic fairy tales, I wondered if you could tell a story inspired by the nursery rhymes that we all learned as young children. I chose Little Miss Muffet because I thought spiders were creepy but fascinating. I'm not afraid of spiders, so I wanted to explore why Miss Muffet was terrified of them to the point that she abandoned her food and fled. Once I had that thought in my head, I couldn't let it go. The Muffets came to life within a matter of weeks. Their trials and adventure with 9958 were a blast to write.

This is one of my favorite books so far. It is my hope that you enjoy reading this book as much as I enjoyed writing it; and that you never underestimate what you encounter in life. Even an expert can be taken by surprise.

About the Author

C.R. Garmen developed her passion for writing at a young age. Starting with retelling the story of three little pigs, she went on to dream of being an author one day. Born and raised in the suburbs of Detroit, she is very close to her family, especially her younger siblings who light up her world and continue to support and fuel her passion for telling stories. Jack of all trades, master of none; C.R. Garmen dabbles in every genre, finding that each one is just a new challenge to explore and take on.

Follow her on Facebook for more updates about new releases.

www.facebook.com/CRGarmen

And check out her blog for some exclusive interviews, new releases, and more!

www.crgarmen.wordpress.com

Printed by Amazon Italia Logistica S.r.l.
Torrazza Piemonte (TO), Italy